WILLIAM MEIKLE

TORMENTOR

Cover art by Zach McCain

First Crossroad Press Edition - 2023

To Sue.
Without her I'd still be scratching stick figures.

Acknowledgments

A big thank-you to the people of Skye, some of the friendliest folks I've met, on one of the most beautiful places on Earth.

FOR SALE

THE SPANIARDS' COTTAGE—Nr. DUNVEGAN, ISLE OF SKYE

Recently renovated detached single-story cottage situated near the community of Dunvegan on the shore of the remote and beautiful Loch Dunvegan, with one bedroom, shower room/water closet and open plan lounge/kitchen/ dining room. The property benefits from a recent modernization of both its electrical system and its plumbing, and has modern fittings throughout while retaining much of its rustic charm from its long and varied history.

The ruined crofter's cottage on the shoreline to the north and the nearby barn both lie within the owner's title.

The area offers inspiring views, rugged landscapes, and a general sense of seclusion. There is a primary school and local amenities in Dunvegan village, where there are also several hotels, a grocery shop and a post office alongside seasonal shopping catering to a brisk tourist trade centered round Dunvegan Castle.

OFFERS OVER £105,000

Viewing can be arranged through David Bean and Sons, Solicitors, Portree, Isle of Skye.

PART 1: KEY

1

As funerals go, it wasn't a bad one.

Nobody fell, wailing on the coffin in the crematorium, nobody cocked up the speech; everybody present—and that was quite a number—said what a lovely girl Beth had been, and how she would be missed. A lot of people asked me how I was holding up, and I didn't swear in my replies. When everybody else had gone, I got a nice little urn that didn't feel heavy at all, and a ride home in the back of a posh car.

Home. That was a word that didn't mean much any more. Not with her gone from it. I held my shit together long enough to get back there, and even managed to pack several boxes of books— alphabetical order, the way she'd have wanted it—before the wall I'd built against the day came down. I sat on the floor amid the cardboard boxes that were all that remained of my life, and wept.

Cancer is too small a word for the thing that destroyed so much, so quickly.

It was there when I scrubbed her back. She had a bad day at work and got a treat—a bottle of wine, some chocolate—and a tumor. I found a lump, no bigger than a pea, nestled up close to her right armpit.

I went with her to see the doctor the next day, then we did the round of tests, more tests and finally diagnosis but by then we both knew it wasn't good news. The cancer was hungry, ravenously so, and it ate her in just over three weeks—twenty-three days to consume sixty kilos of fat, muscle, blood, tissue, and one life, barely used.

3

Beth fought it every inch of the way, with all her heart, which was considerable. She raged, she swore and she endured; radiotherapy first, chemo almost straightaway after. Her hair fell out in clumps, her eyes fell back in her skull into shadowy pits, and her arms when they held me were like thin, dry sticks. She fought harder. She was strong.

The cancer was stronger. She slipped away from me ,in a morphine haze, and I'm not even sure she knew who I was at the end. Around eight o'clock in the evening, five days short of her twenty-eighth birthday, I held her hand as the machines stopped beeping.

Three years—that's what we had. It was never going to be enough.

There are two things you need to know about me—firstly, I'm what they used to call "independently wealthy." Dad was in shipping—lots of shipping. He loved to tell everyone he was a self-made millionaire, ten times over. I never really knew how much money he earned—or spent—all I knew was that I had very little contact with him during my childhood in a variety of boarding schools. His heart gave out when I was fifteen, almost two years to the day from the last time I'd seen him. I got a trust fund that set me up for life, Mom got a new man—I got the better of the deal.

The money meant university was stress free, and I could take my time choosing a job. Rather too much time, as it turned out, but two years in the Med pretending to be an artist left me with plenty of memories to carry forward. A chance interview where I and the guy across the desk just seemed to click meant I started a job in IT in London only three weeks after getting back. A week after that I met Beth—and you already know what happened there.

The second thing you don't know is that I'm a runner; it happens whenever I get stressed. Some people buckle, some work harder, but I'm a quitter—always have been, since back before puberty. I hide with my hands over my eyes until it's safe to come back out again. I'm not proud of it, but it's hard-wired, and it's an impulse I always have to push against.

For the two years after Beth died, I pushed, trying to keep my act together, because that's what she would have wanted. I struggled, but one day I looked up and things seemed a bit clearer, a bit less bleak. People started to talk to me like a human being; I even socialized occasionally. But after three months of being a normal person again, I came to the realization that I no longer gave a shit about the job, or London, or any of the things I'd been working so hard to keep together. I looked at my bank account, looked out instead of in, and ran.

All of the above is by way of preamble—necessary background I thought I should get out of the way early on to save having to explain myself later. I don't want to waste much more time talking about me.

This story isn't really about me. I want to tell you about the place I ran to.

This is the story of a house.

2

Beth was always a city girl through and through, born and bred in London with little thought for how life was lived anywhere else. She'd never had fantasies about escaping to the countryside and getting away from it all; she loved the hustle and bustle of the city too much. She needed her coffee, her cinemas, shops, bright lights and nightlife. She wanted to be able to call up friends and be in a bar ten minutes later, or to take a visit to the V&A and eat in Harrods at the drop of a hat.

While I was with her, I needed those things too, but without her London seemed pointless—a mound full of termites running around doing things that benefited other termites and pretending it mattered a jot.

Growing up in boarding schools hadn't been too bad. I remembered big skies, rolling hills, farmers and the smell of manure, clear flowing rivers and tall trees. I wanted that again, that sense of youth. When I run, I don't do things by halves. Barely a month after making my decision, I moved into the house by a sea loch in Skye.

I chose a shoreline because of a childhood memory of clambering through rock pools, chose the island because I'd always liked the name and the history it evoked, and chose the house because when I saw the picture on the estate agents' website, it spoke straight to my soul. I didn't even bother paying a visit before buying it—I was living on instinct.

But on the day I got the keys and moved my stuff in, I knew I'd done the right thing.

Tormentor

It was early May—spring, almost summer back in London, but up here it was still late winter, with snow clinging to the tops of the hills and some slushy ice in the harbor at the foot of the slope by the kitchen door.

Alan Bean showed me around. We'd talked a lot on the phone over the last few weeks as he untangled the mess of paperwork that goes with buying an old property. From his manner on the phone I'd imagined a stocky, almost portly man, middle-aged maybe, but Alan was younger than me—also three inches taller and a little lighter.

"This lanky streak of pish is my son, Alan," his father had said as he'd introduced us. Alan shook my hand.

"Jim, Jim Greenwood," I said. He smiled and I knew straightaway—I'd found a friend.

I had followed his car over the winding coastal road from Portree, then up the rutted track that was euphemistically known as "the private road." We got out of our respective cars and stood outside the cottage for my first look around.

From this vantage point the view was completely wild—no roads or pylons visible, no other houses, just the loch, with wavelets slightly churning in a stiff breeze, the purple hills hanging in a haze across the water and white clouds scudding north across the sky.

The house itself was unremarkable from the outside—four white-washed walls and a slate-tiled roof, a window on either side of a door placed slightly off center, giving the structure a slightly quizzical demeanor. A ruined crofter's cottage sat twenty yards away on the shore to the west. We had parked the cars in a stone enclosure to the south I knew at one time had been a barn, reduced now to three good walls, and open to the elements above.

"I don't normally come out on moving day," Alan said as we walked toward the main building. "But nobody's ever bought a house from me, sight-unseen, before today."

I laughed, and it felt natural and right, so I did it again.

"I took the web tour," I said. "Welcome to the twenty-first century."

Alan laughed with me.

"This is Skye—we've only just come out of the nineteenth around here. And in some places, even that is seen as too modern."

I patted the barn wall on the way past.

"Just how old is this?" I asked.

"The barn is nineteenth century, the crofter's cottage about the same. The main house is anybody's guess—some say the name came from a shipwrecked crew from an armada galleon trying to take the long way home—but there are even older stories about the place if you believe the locals. I'll let you find that out for yourself— you'll need something to talk about in the bar."

The main room of my new home had little sense of the kind of age Alan had just described. The front door opened into a small porch, then straight into a long open area that took up half the house. There were new hardwood floors, exposed beams and rough stonework, but it all looked like it had been put together yesterday, and even the large granite fireplace had been scrubbed clean of any soot that might have built up over the years.

Alan saw me looking.

"Mrs. Menzies was a bit obsessive about dirt," he said. "I've never seen a cleaner house."

"I'm sure I can do something about that," I said, and smiled.

The movers had been and gone, and the sum of my belongings—apart from a new bed, a sofa, a cooker and a fridge that had also been delivered that morning—were huddled in a small sad group of boxes and suitcases in the center of the floor.

Alan raised an eyebrow.

"Traveling light?"

"I brought what I thought I'd need," I said—but in truth, I'd only brought things that wouldn't remind me too much of Beth.

"Well, so did I," Alan replied. "I'll be back."

8

Tormentor

He left me alone for several minutes, and I had my first impression of what this place was going to be like for me—even in that short time, I felt the emptiness start to close in, the silence creeping. I was looking forward to it.

Alan returned and handed me a long box containing a bottle of Talisker single malt.

"This is the local firewater," he said. "Treat it with love and care, and it'll serve you well in cold nights to come."

"Will you have one with me—to christen the house?"

A look I didn't understand crossed his face, quickly wiped away with a smile.

"Just a wee one, then, if you insist. I have to drive back to Portree."

It took me ten minutes to find the glasses—they were packed away in the same box as Beth's ashes, and I wasn't able to prevent Alan from getting a look at the urn. He was too good a man to say anything right then, but I had a feeling the conversation was now inevitable at some point in our future.

The Scotch was stronger than I'd anticipated, and I'm afraid it caused me to splutter on the first sip.

Alan laughed loudly.

"Dinna worry, man. You'll get the hang of it soon enough."

He was as good as his word and only had one small glass—a single finger at most, then he was off and away leaving me with an empty house and a load of boxes I had no urge to unpack.

A pair of French doors dominated the west-facing side of the room, and led from the dining room out to a small paved patio. I made myself a coffee and took it—and another small glass of the Scotch, outside. The garden furniture on the patio was cast iron and solid—freezing cold on the buttocks to start with, but surprisingly comfortable once I got settled. I was more than aware of the cold wind off the sea, but it was not too hard to bear, and I sat there for some time, sipping alternately from coffee and whisky, and letting the quiet fill me up.

My stillness served to embolden some of the other inhabitants—a stoat, just losing its ermine, poked its head out from a pile of firewood down by the ruined cottage and just as quickly turned away. A pair of sparrows briefly touched down—in case I had any crumbs to spare—and out in the loch a seal bobbed up to check me out before diving away. There was no traffic noise, no music. There was just the lap of water on rock and the whistle of the wind in my ears.

I felt more alive than at any time since Beth's passing.

I spent the rest of the afternoon doing some halfhearted unpacking—essentials like stereo system and laptop first—but after putting Beth's urn on the huge stone mantel above the fire I lost the heart for it. I'd had enough foresight to bring some basic food supplies and, after taking a good ten minutes to figure out the new cooker, I was able to throw together a basic meal of rice, fish and vegetables that seemed much better than anything I'd ever eaten in the city.

I got the laptop fired up. Internet usage was going to be expensive, having to be accessed through my phone and a dongle, but I wasn't anticipating much need for it anyway. I found a small folding table in the pantry when I was putting the food away, and sat the laptop on it in front of the sofa. I chose one of the movies I had on the hard drive and lay on the sofa watching the U.S. military fight off an alien invasion. The plot was set on Earth, but may as well have been on another planet entirely—I was a long way away from Hollywood's idea of civilization.

I was also starting to realize how much I was going to need—a work desk and chair for a start, and probably a washing machine, unless I wanted to spend my time bent over the butler's sink in the kitchen. Then there were the practicalities—meter readings, septic tank emptying (something I promised myself I wouldn't forget), council tax payments, bank statements and all the other small bureaucratic hoops that needed to be jumped through. I'd already dealt with a lot of the more pressing issues, but the speed with which I made the move would inevitably lead to some loose ends if I didn't get to it soon.

After the film finished, I started to make a list of things to do the next day—it took longer than I thought, and by the time I was finished I was surprised to look up and see it was almost full dark outside.

I made another coffee, poured another Scotch, and went out to see my new view at night.

It was immediately obvious I needed to add a flashlight to my list. It was a moonless night, and when I looked up I saw no stars; it had clouded over since earlier. Several lights showed on the far shore of the loch—far-apart, solitary dwellings at a guess. Out on the middle of the sound a red light flashed—a marker buoy of some kind—another guess. Water lapped on the old stone in the small harbor down to my left, but I could see nothing but shifting darkness down there. What little light came through from the dining room and out the doors only lit up the immediate area around the iron table and chairs. The ruined crofter's cottage was merely a darker blob in the shadows, and I couldn't make out the woodpile at all.

In the same spot where I had felt calm, almost serene that same afternoon, the air now felt heavy and oppressive, the darkness taking on the heft and weight of something alive.

I retreated indoors, got another Scotch and watched another film on the laptop, trying not to think of the shadows that even now peered in the French windows. When I got up for another drink, I added curtains to my shopping list.

3

I had a restless night, not yet acclimated to the creaks and groans of a new place, and disconcerted by the play of light and shadow in my bedroom caused by the moon's reflections off the loch and fast clouds scudding overhead. When I started to imagine figures peering at me from the shadows, I resorted to hiding under the blankets, eyes firmly closed.

First thing in the morning, I amended the last item on my list to "more curtains," had a quick breakfast of coffee and toast, then headed for Portree to do some shopping. I took my time on the drive. Although it was still cloudy, it was dry and with the windows rolled down I smelled the sea—and, yes, manure, at every turn of the road.

It was midmorning before I pulled up in the town square parking area, and past noon before I managed to tick off the items on my list. I'd underestimated the difficulty of getting what I wanted this far away from the larger stores on the mainland. I was going to have to wait for a writing desk and chair, and the washing machine would be a week's wait for delivery. I did, however, get a powerful flashlight, and curtains.

I stocked up on beer at the off license and by the time I was ready to leave, the trunk of the car was full, my shopping spilling over into the rear seats. I had just organized it all to my liking when I heard Alan Bean speak from behind me.

"So, you needed more than you thought you did then?"

"Just a bit," I said, laughing.

"It's my lunch hour," he said. "Do you have time for a bite?"

I thought he might lead me to a café or restaurant, but instead I followed him for ten yards, straight into the public bar of the George Hotel, where he ordered two beers.

"Just the one," I said, echoing his words from the day before. "I'm driving. And I've got curtains to put up."

"Living the high life already, I see?" he replied. He handed me a beer that looked far darker than I was used to down south. It tasted stronger too—full of malt and caramel. It went down smoothly enough though.

"Settling in okay?" he asked after we'd ordered some sandwiches and taken a seat in the corner.

"You know what it's like," I said. "New house, new place and too much quiet—I didn't get much sleep."

"That's what the Talisker was meant for," he said, and laughed. "You'll soon get used to the quiet, and if you want some noise, come down here on a Saturday night, or over to the Dunvegan Arms, your new local. It gets a bit lively in the summer over there."

I hadn't paid much attention to what he was saying. An old woman—somewhere in her eighties by the looks of her—hadn't taken her eyes off me since I sat down. It looked like the man with her—her son probably—was trying to get her to stop staring, but he wasn't having any luck with that.

Alan saw me looking and turned. That was her cue to start talking, too loud in what had until then been a quiet bar.

"You should be ashamed of yourself, Alan Bean—selling that house after what it did to poor Annie Menzies."

Her son stood and got the woman out of her seat.

"Sorry Alan," he said. "You know what she's like…"

"Ashamed!" she shouted, and by now the whole bar was watching the performance. "It should have been burned down, like in the old times. No good will come of it—we all know that."

With another "sorry," the man got her out of the door, but not without a parting shout from her.

"Burn it down. Burn it and pish on the ashes—do it now, before it's too late."

The door swung closed behind them, and the rest of the bar went back to their conversations.

"What the hell was that all about?"

Alan didn't seem perturbed.

"The auld dear has gone a bit off-kilter these past few years—Alzheimer's or so I've heard—she doesn't mean anything by it."

"Just tell me I haven't bought myself the proverbial local bad place. I'm not going to have kids coming round looking for spooks, am I?"

"Och, no, man," he replied. "There's not a house on the island that doesn't have a story attached—and yours is older than most. Just think of it this way, there's more happy stories than there are sad over the centuries, a few bad years doesn't make a bad house."

The sandwiches arrived and our conversation turned to mundane matters. I found out where to pay my taxes, got a good contact for a contractor to look after the septic tank, then turned down the offer of a second beer.

"Another time," I said. "When neither of us are driving. We'll sink a few and bring me up to speed on the stories—all of them. It'll be nice to know the full history of the place."

Once again a strange look passed across Alan's face, but I scarcely noticed, for the smile replaced it as quickly as before.

"We have a date then," he said.

We shook hands as we parted in the car park. As I turned back to my car, I saw the old lady and her son standing in the far corner. This time both of them were staring at me, but thankfully there was no more shouting.

The first thing I did upon getting back to the cottage was to put up the curtains. I felt faintly ridiculous, preparing myself for a siege against the shadows was how I thought of it, until the thought itself caused me to laugh out loud. I did, however, immediately feel less nervous about the coming night, so I counted it as a good result once the curtains were hanging in place. I made myself a coffee and took it out to the patio—I had a feeling this was going to become a ritual.

I was still slightly on edge, as the old lady's outburst was hard to ignore, despite Alan's measured denial of anything untoward. I've never paid much attention to stories of spooks and haunts—that was one of Beth's things I didn't share—but I didn't really fancy being the incoming tenant that got shunned by the locals purely because of where I lived.

Once again a combination of coffee and the view did its job of calming me down, and I resolved I'd get myself down to Dunvegan soon and begin introducing myself to my neighbors, distant though they may be.

There was a different feel to the view again—clear skies and not even a flicker of a breeze, the loch sitting flat calm, like a piece of glass topped with the thinnest of thin layers of water. The friendly sparrows came and checked me out. I made a mental note to add some bird feeders to my shopping list, and down by the firewood the stoat showed me its tail as it fled when I spotted it.

I went inside to rustle up some early supper, all thoughts of the old lady's warnings driven away.

In the early evening I checked my email. I had three requests from my old job that could safely be ignored and two notes from pals back in the city wondering if I'd gone native yet. There was also a heap of spam, and one very peculiar item that looked like it might have been in English at one time but was now mangled and corrupted. I put it down to a fault at the sender's end and deleted it.

I spent an hour or so doing more unpacking. I got as far as getting my easel and paints out, which meant I was as close to doing any actual painting as I'd been for several years, but that was as far as it went. I fully intended for the painting to be my main thing, something I'd always aspired to but hadn't done anything about since playing at it in the Med before meeting Beth. I was hoping the solitude and quiet, not to mention the views, would inspire me into action. But for now, everything was just too new, too exciting. I made another coffee and went outside to watch the sun go down over the far side of the loch. I only went back in as the stars came out and the chill became too much to bear.

4

That first week passed quickly.

I finished unpacking and set about getting the house the way I wanted it. My desk and chair arrived the same morning as the new washing machine, in the same van. The driver was rather taciturn, and when he did speak, his accent was so thick as to be almost impenetrable. He refused a tip, and seemed rather too eager to be off and away, to the extent that I was left to plumb in the washing machine myself.

After that first night, the darkness and shifting shadows had ceased to worry me, and I even took to opening my bedroom curtains just so I could watch the interplay on the ceiling while dozing off—like a kid with a night-light. I was sleeping better than I'd ever managed in London; my head felt clear and alert. My coffee vigils on the patio were quickly becoming the highlight of my days. The sparrows encroached ever closer, the stoat had taken to sitting on top of the woodpile and trying to stare me out, and several seals regularly hauled themselves out on the rocks along the shoreline.

I made my first trip as far along as the old crofter's cottage during an attempt to catch a photograph of the seals. I was far too clumsy and loud to sneak up on the animals, and they made a dive into the water before I got anywhere near close enough for a photo, but by then my whole attention was on the old cottage in any case.

I owned it—that much I knew. Alan had also told me it was abandoned sometime more than fifty years previous, but that was all he'd known. It was smaller than I had imagined—barely twelve feet on a side and little more than a box with a roof with two tiny windows, only a foot square, set on the side facing the sea. A rotting wooden door hung off its hinges, and I wasn't sure if I was too keen on seeing what lay inside.

But it was my property—it had been for a week now, and I still hadn't seen it. It would give Alan a laugh at least if he knew I was so recalcitrant about entering. I pushed open the door, not knowing what to expect.

There was nothing to see, just four bare walls, blackened by soot from a long-dead fire. The place had been emptied at some point after its scorching—*scoured* would be a better word, for there was no sign of furniture, fixtures or fittings, just stone walls and dirt floor. The roof, what little was left of it, sagged badly in places and looked like it might not last long in a strong wind. I was about to turn away when a cloud shifted and the sun came out, lighting up, only for a second, the wall that sat deepest in shadow. There was faded writing, in four-inch-high letters, done with the end of a finger in the ash.

It was just two words.

Stay down.

I decided that Saturday to take Alan's advice and check out the local hotel. I walked down to Dunvegan—three miles of dirt track along the side of the loch, a most pleasant stroll in the cool evening with the sun starting its descent in the west and a light breeze playing on the water. I didn't see a single soul until I turned the corner to look over the old castle where a busload of tourists was getting ready to leave.

The bus passed me as I walked down the avenue of chestnuts and sycamores leading from the castle into the village itself, and I arrived at the Dunvegan Arms to find them all ahead of me in the lounge bar. Given the length of the line, I was about to turn around and try another hotel when a small man poked his head round a door.

"In here," he said. "The grockles don't know about this one."

I followed him through into a much smaller, but cozier, bar area—obviously one for the locals judging by the clientele.

"Thanks," I said to my savior. "Can I get you a beer?"

I quickly found out those are not the best words to say to a Skye local with a thirst. He kept me company for the next hour, and I was three pints poorer when he left. He also knew a damn sight more about me than I would have thought.

"You're the mannie that bought the Spaniards' place, aren't you?" he asked as the first beer went down. He kept up an almost constant flow of chatter, about people I hadn't met yet, about the problems of local farmers, and about how I was going to love the place. He'd left for home before I realized he had adeptly fielded every single one of my questions that might have led to any discussion about the house itself or its history.

Over the course of the evening in the bar, I started to see a pattern emerging. The locals were unfailingly friendly, open and instantly charming, and none of them would tell me anything at all about the history of the house I'd bought. Every attempt to start that conversation was steered, most politely and often in a roundabout manner, toward a different subject. If the intent was to reassure me in any way, it did exactly the opposite.

Alan had been right about the hotel though. Things got decidedly lively as the night wore on, but I took my leave when a country and western trio started up in the main lounge, their volume turned up so high that any further quiet conversation was well-nigh impossible.

The strains of "Stand by Your Man" followed me as I headed up the avenue toward the castle and the shore path beyond.

The walk back was almost as pleasant as the earlier one had been. The night air felt chilly, but with a hint that summer might eventually be arriving, even here. There was enough light for me to see the track, most of the time, but I resolved to bring the flashlight the next time.

It also took me longer to get back than I anticipated, so I was relieved when I saw the squat shape of the house on the horizon, a darker shadow against the sky. I was less happy to see the light was on in the main room, for I had a distinct memory of switching it off before I left.

There were no cars but mine in the barn or driveway, and no sound from inside. I went in the front door, noisily, to let anyone who might be there know of my presence.

"Hello?" I shouted, then immediately felt self-conscious...and stupid. Beth and I had often jeered at movies when people did exactly the same thing. If there is indeed a prowler present, he's hardly going to shout back, *"Yes, I'm just lurking in the closet with a big knife."*

Thankfully my stupidity went unnoticed; there was no reply. I did a tour of the house. The French windows were securely locked, there was no sign of anything missing, and I started to think my memory was playing tricks when it came to switching off the lights.

Then I saw my laptop.

The lid was open and the machine switched on, sitting on top of the new desk. By now I was worried more about my sanity than my memory, for I was absolutely certain I'd powered it down before leaving.

I had new email—two items, both scrambled gibberish, but both containing two words that were all too clear.

Stay down.

Tormentor

A restless night followed. I couldn't settle, worried by the fact that someone might have been in the house, and almost equally worried it was my own mind playing tricks on me. I chased down the beer I'd had earlier with a few more from the fridge and tried to wash my mind clear with a big dumb action movie on the laptop. It didn't work. Even epic-sized Hollywood bangs weren't enough to drive away a growing unease. I thought about following the beer down with some of the Talisker, but that would have felt too much like giving in. Instead I turned to something I hadn't done since the week after the funeral—I talked to Beth. Or rather, I talked to the urn, for in my heart I knew it was all that was left of her—there was no happier place beyond, no celestial harps. Not for Beth, or for me. If there were anything of her left, she'd have talked to me before now.

"I'm going mad, sweetheart," I whispered.

I could well imagine her reply. She didn't have to be here for me to know exactly what it would be.

"What, again?"

But just giving voice to my fears seemed to do the trick. Hearing them spoken aloud diminished them; it brought them into focus and made me see them for what they were—new-house nerves and fear of change.

I went to bed feeling less nervous, and fell asleep watching the patterns of light and shadow on the ceiling coming in through the curtains I deliberately left open—my small gesture of defiance, one I needed that night to prove to myself I wasn't afraid of the dark.

5

By the time June came around I'd settled into a routine. I painted, or at least thought about painting during the day, and watched movies on the laptop at night. I took to having regular coffee breaks out on the patio and spent Saturday evenings in the Dunvegan Arms where I was almost getting treated as a regular, if not yet one of the locals. I still couldn't get anyone to talk to me about the house's history though, but that seemed less important now, given there had been no recurrence of the strange emails and no sign of any nocturnal intruders.

I was starting to feel like I had found a new home, somewhere I could settle.

On the second of the month, I had to go into Portree to pay my council tax, so I took the opportunity to visit Alan Bean. He was only too happy to be invited to lunch.

"I need a break. I've been wrangling with the land register over an old farm property all morning," he said. "Some of this stuff goes back to Bonnie Prince Charlie's day, and, around here at least, they bought and sold land like they were lending and borrowing books from a library. It's a bloody mess."

He stood from his desk and stretched.

"It might be a long one," he said to his secretary—a small, timid-looking girl who couldn't be long out of school—and led me out into the main square. We didn't head for the George this time, but around past the harbor wall to a more modern restaurant perched on a corner of the Uig road. There was a line of what looked like tourists waiting for a table, but Alan waved at one of the waiters and we were shown to a window seat with a view out over the fishing boats to the hills beyond. It was one of those days where you wouldn't want to be anywhere else—turquoise sky with fluffy white clouds, a slight breeze on the water and gulls doing aerobatics overhead.

Alan saw me looking.

"So you're not regretting coming then?"

"Not for a second," I replied.

The waiter interrupted any further conversation by bringing a menu.

"I can recommend the Chicken Jalfrezi. My treat," Alan said. "I'll slip it past Dad on expenses. And they've got some fine island beers on tap too."

The curry proved to be very good indeed, fiery yet subtle, and the ale, a local wheat beer, complemented it perfectly. Alan's conversation danced over the top of both, always lively and humorous, with an underlying sarcasm that suited my temperament. He told me of the happenings on the island, and I told him what little there was to tell of my first month.

I wasn't going to mention it, but I did let slip about the writing on the wall in the old cottage, and the two words I'd read both there and in my emails.

"Kids, most likely," he said. "They're always on the lookout for somewhere to have a quiet smoke away from the eyes of their parents."

I wasn't convinced—not at all—but Alan was such a convivial companion, and it didn't feel like an issue worth arguing over, so I let it drop, and conversation quickly turned to the Dunvegan Arms.

"How are they treating you?" Alan asked.

"Very well," I replied. "They're a talkative bunch, when it suits them."

He picked up on my sarcasm. "Don't push it, Jim," he said quietly. "Yes, they like to talk—we all do over here. It's our favorite pastime, after sex of course, but there's only so many times you can look at a sheep.

"We all keep secrets. I'm sure you've got some of your own. Just relax, enjoy your house, and trust me, there's nothing you need to know that'll help you in the knowing of it."

I let it lie—it was a niggle, but no more than that, and not enough of one to be worth too much attention. Alan had a second beer and I had a coffee, aware of the forty-five-minute drive I still had ahead of me to get home. He looked like he was just getting started.

"Come down in a taxi sometime," Alan said, as we parted in midafternoon. "We can make a day of it, have a few beers—more than a few beers—and maybe if you get me drunk enough, I'll tell you some of those stories you seem so keen on hearing."

I laughed.

"If I wait until you're drunk enough, I'll be comatose myself and long past being capable of listening."

He grinned.

"As if that would stop me."

We shook hands, and he went back to his musty files and land registry history. I turned away to head for my car...and realized I was being watched.

They were over in the far corner of the car park again—the old woman and her son, just standing, staring at me. Back in London I'd have got in the car and driven off, feeling slightly intimidated, if not even fearful, but I'd come up here to be master of my own destiny. After such a pleasant lunch, I wasn't in the mood to have the afternoon ruined by any bullshit.

I walked over, slowly, half expecting them to back off, hoping to embarrass them into silence. It didn't work—but at least the old lady had lost her belligerence from our earlier encounter in the bar.

"You should leave, son," she said softly. "You're not safe here."

"Is that a threat?"

She smiled, and suddenly looked much younger.

"Don't be daft, laddie. I'm trying to help you. No good will come of staying in that place. It drove my old pal mad in the end, trying to keep them out."

"Keep who out? Speak sense, will you?"

"If you don't know yet, you will soon," she said. "They don't stay down for long."

I was so stunned to hear those words, I only stood, mouth flapping, and watched the man lead his mother away.

What had been merely a niggle had quickly come back as a fully-fledged worry.

I considered getting the truth out of Alan once and for all, but when I turned and looked in the Bean and Sons' office window, he was at his desk, head down in paperwork.

I got in the car and drove, not paying much attention to the scenery on the way back. My mind was full of a tangle of words and images—the finger-writing on the wall, the old lady with her false teeth loose in her gums as she gave me a warning, and Alan's ready smile as he told me there was nothing to worry about.

Upon reaching the house, I went straight to the kitchen, fetched a pail of water and a sponge and went out to the ruined cottage, intending to wash the offending words away, as if that would cleanse them from my mind. I pushed open the old door, walked into the empty room, and stared, openmouthed again, at four blank walls. The soot and ash was still there, and the room still looked like it had been scoured, but there was no writing, and no sign there had ever been any.

I studied the wall from every possible angle, even putting my cheek against it and sighting along its length, but to no avail. All I got was a sooty spot on my face, and more of it on my fingers when I tried to rub it away.

I backed away to the door and tried to create a different shadow inside the room by opening and closing it, but there was still no writing. In the end I threw the pail of water at the wall anyway, standing there as it left dark running streaks pooling in even darker puddles on the floor. I slammed the door as I left—not quite enough to break it off its hinges, but enough that it hung there precariously, creaking in the breeze behind me like mocking laughter.

I caught a glimpse of myself in the mirror as I went back inside; a long streak of soot ran down my left cheek, from just below the eye socket to my chin. It looked like a thin finger had drawn it there.

It took me several minutes to wash it off. The soot and ash felt sticky, almost oily to the touch and resisted first a facecloth and then enough soap to wash a family before finally being defeated. The facecloth in particular came off second best. It had been white when I picked it up, but was now a flat gray, mottled with darker spots as if a fungal disease had taken hold on the surface.

I tossed the cloth into the washing machine and headed for the booze, skipping the intermediary beer and going straight for Scotch. I stood at the patio doors, looking over toward the ruined cottage. It was still just four walls and a roof, but now it had taken on a new role—tormentor. I made a mental note to talk to Alan about whether I could just pull it down—raze it to the ground and piss on the rubble—then pulled the curtains closed, shutting it out. The view didn't appeal to me right then.

I went to the laptop, looking for another movie to lose myself in. The machine was open—not unusual in itself, as I'd taken to leaving it plugged in, on top of the desk. It was also switched on—again, not too unusual as I often wandered away and left it that way.

What was unusual was the finger-thin streak of soot running down the screen. I hadn't been anywhere near it since coming back

26

inside. I used a handkerchief this time, and a dab of the Scotch, and thankfully it wiped away without leaving a smear. As I knocked back what was left of the liquor and turned to pour another, my inbox pinged.

I had three emails, all garbled text. In all three there were only two discernible words.

Stay down.

6

I kept my distance from the crofter's cottage for several weeks afterward, although I did not let it damage my coffee ritual, which was fast becoming a habit. One fine morning, almost two weeks after my last trip to Portree, I was sitting outside with a coffee and a book when I heard the sound of a vehicle approaching up the track, wheels spinning in the dry dirt and gravel. I walked round to the barn just in time to see Alan Bean park an SUV with a dinghy on a trailer behind it.

"It's time to start your long conversion into a man of the isles," he said as he disembarked. "And it starts with fishing."

"I've never fished. And I've never been out in anything bigger than a paddleboat in the Med," I said, laughing.

He smiled.

"Not much difference here then," he said. "Apart from the cold water, the lack of sun, and the complete absence of bikini-clad blondes. I do have one saving factor."

He opened the trunk of the SUV. Alongside the rods and tackle was a twelve-bottle pack of strong local ale.

"Can you get done for being drunk in charge of a dinghy?" I asked as I helped him, first with reversing the trailer down to the small harbor below the kitchen window, then with getting the dinghy loaded and into the water.

"Who said anything about you being in charge?" he replied. "And it's 'Captain Alan, sir,' to you for the duration."

"Aye, aye, Captain Alan, sir," I replied, and saluted.

"Cast off at the blunt end," he shouted, and started up the outboard motor.

The next few hours stay etched in my mind—a clear, perfect moment summing up everything good about my new home. We cruised up and down the loch, trailing fishing lines behind us that contained little more than hooks and splashes of colored thread at six-inch intervals along the length.

"No need for any fancy bait today. We're after the mackerel." Alan said. "They're like teenagers—unable to resist anything shiny passing into their view."

He was proven right even before we got through the first beer. I hadn't spotted any bending or jerking of the stiff rods we were using, but when we brought in the lines, we each had a full load of black and silver fish—a dozen in total in our first haul alone.

"I hope you've got plenty of room in your freezer," Alan said. "It looks like a day for a big catch."

Yet again he was proven right. Over the next hour or so we brought in over a hundred fish and drank three beers each. I even piloted the dinghy for a spell, although my attempts at turning only brought hysterical laughter from Alan.

"We'll take things slowly, shall we," he said, taking the tiller from me.

All in all, it was a glorious way to spend the morning.

Alan wasn't finished with my education. Once back in the house we filled one of the two butler's sinks with the fish.

"Now comes the icky part. What do you want to do—heads or guts?"

I must have looked bemused for he laughed loudly again.

"Watch and learn," he said.

He lifted the first fish and lopped off its head with one slice of my heaviest knife, sliding the severed head into the empty sink and putting the rest of the fish to one side.

"That's your job, then you pass them to me and I'll clean them out."

I quickly discovered what he meant by *icky*—within minutes the second sink was filling up with heads and guts, and over at the table Alan had laid out a line of gutted fish I wasn't sure I'd ever be able to eat.

Some accompanying beer made the job more palatable though, and Alan seemed happy in his work. He even cleaned up most of the resultant mess when we were done.

Over the course of the afternoon we made several pounds of mackerel pate—cooked fish, butter and pepper in the main, blitzed in a blender and put in the fridge to chill. We stuffed freezer bags full of the remaining fish—all apart from six, which Alan grilled with some butter, garlic and herbs and we ate out on the patio with the remainder of the beer to wash it down. I was as relaxed as I'd been at any time since my arrival on the island.

"You seem to be settling in okay," Alan said. "I thought you would, although I hear you had another run-in with auld Mrs. Duncan that last day in Portree. I hope she didn't upset you."

I happened to be looking at the crofter's cottage as he spoke, and as if a switch had been pulled, all the goodness drained out of the day.

Alan saw me looking, and his smile disappeared.

"What did she tell you?"

"Nothing at all, just some stuff about the old lady who lived here before."

"Mrs. Menzies? Aye, it was sad the way she went at the end. But old people die—there's no need to make up supernatural melodramas about it, although I admit making up stories is a bit of a local pastime around here."

"It's not just that…" I started. "It's that old crofter's cottage — it's got me spooked."

"It's that auld busybody that's got you spooked. I suppose it's about time you knew what's got her back up, but I'll need a few drinks to tell the full story, if you don't mind me kipping on your couch tonight?"

"If it gets everything out and into the open, that's fine by me."

I fetched us both some beer from my stock in the fridge and went back out onto the patio. The sun was making its way overhead and we sat in sunlight, a cool breeze blowing in from the sea.

"I didn't want to tell you any of this stuff," he started. "Not right away at least, not until I knew you were settled and saw for yourself there was nothing in the stories to be worried about."

He took a long gulp of beer.

"Mrs. Menzies bought the place back in the Sixties. In fact, it was Dad who sold it to her and her husband. I remember him, just. Nice chap, kept himself to himself; Mrs. Menzies did enough talking for the two of them. He died in the early Eighties, nothing suspicious, a dicky ticker and too many fags seemed to be the general consensus among the gossiping classes. Mrs. Menzies went a bit strange soon after that. If we're to believe the tittle-tattle, it all started with the soot."

That made me jump, the involuntary twitch causing me to spill beer on the patio slabs beneath me.

Alan laughed.

"You've only been here a few weeks and you've got a drinking problem already. Did I say something wrong?"

I motioned for him to go on as I dabbed at a damp spot on my trousers with a handkerchief. I wasn't ready yet to tell him about the writing; I wondered if I ever would be ready. He took a long sip of his beer before continuing.

"Anyway, back to Mrs. Menzies. She started to make complaints about neighbors burning bonfires and getting soot on her washing. As you can see for yourself, there are no neighbors close enough for smoke to be a concern. But she was adamant and caused quite a stooshie in the shop in Dunvegan when she started hitting Mr. Hannah over the head with her umbrella, shouting about him persecuting her and sneaking about among her underwear and nightgowns.

"Things got worse when she filed numerous police reports about intruders getting into her house and making a mess. I've got a pal, Detective John Thompson, who was a bobby at the time, and he was called out time and time again. He said all they ever found was a wee bit of soot here and there, and he suspected Mrs. Menzies of doing it herself, for they never found any sign that anyone else had been in the house.

"She took to cleaning, and I suspect the bulk of her pension went on bleach and detergent by the end. John said the place stank so much it stung one's eyes if you stayed there too long. And she tore the place apart, stripping it down to the bare walls before rebuilding, which incidentally is why you've got all this new electrics and plumbing. Still she wasn't satisfied. The police ignored her calls after a while, but they did send a doctor round, several times. He reported that the old woman was lucid enough, but suffering from several delusions, the main one of which concerned 'ghosts and ghoulies' smearing her house with soot when she wasn't looking."

I must have reacted again, because Alan stopped and raised an eyebrow.

"Are you sure you want to hear this? I don't want to be the cause of any sleepless nights for you."

"I'm fine, but I need another beer."

I went back into the kitchen, more to calm my fraying nerves away from Alan than from any great need for the booze. When I returned with a beer for each of us, he was less keen to continue.

"Look, I can stop there if you like? I meant it when I said it wasn't anything you really needed to know."

"That's just it," I replied. "I think I do need to know, if only to dismiss it. Please, go on."

He took another long chug of beer and continued.

"For a while the situation seemed to have stabilized. Everyone knew the old lady was a bit strange, but her constant cleaning seemed to have solved her main problem. And this is where I come into the story—about two years back.

"We got a phone call, saying she wanted to put the place on the market. Dad sent me out to see her to get things started, and so began one of the strangest afternoons of my life.

"The house was almost exactly as you see it now, with one exception—it did indeed stink of bleach, detergent and God alone knows what else. All the time I was there, which was several hours, she constantly moved around the room, a wee dance that looked almost ritualistic as she wiped and dusted everything, only to start again immediately after she finished. She looked tired, worn out, an old lady running on fumes and nervous energy.

"I had a series of questions I needed to get answered, but it was tough getting a word in edgeways as she kept up a constant stream-of-consciousness chat. I kind of caught the gist as she went along. To cut a long story short, she felt that the spooks were getting stronger, and she feared for her safety if she stayed much longer.

"She also wanted to know if she could have the crofter's old cottage removed completely from the land. I told her it would be a selling point, at which juncture she started laughing uncontrollably and I couldn't get her to stop.

"I left her with a promise to get the ball rolling on a sale, and beat it the hell out of there.

"She was dead two days later."

———————

The statement had come at me too abruptly and I struggled to process it, covering up my confusion by sipping at my beer.

"So, what was it? Just old age?" I asked, hoping for a mundane answer.

Alan wasn't smiling anymore.

"Nobody really knows why she did it, but look, she was old and losing her wits. The fire could have been an accident."

"She burned…and it was out in the crofter's cottage, wasn't it?"

He was having trouble looking me in the eye, obviously feeling guilty.

"I'm afraid so. I should really have told you, but…"

"But it's been two years since her death, no sensible local would touch the place, and you needed to make a sale…I get it." I actually felt relief now that I knew. "It's not that big of a deal, really. Back in London, I lived on top of one of the old plague pits for a while, and I grew up on a house overlooking a cemetery. If spooks were going to plague me, they'd have done it long ago. Trust me. I'm fine."

"Really?"

"Yes, really," I replied. I tried to feel like I meant it.

"Really, really," he said in a perfect impersonation of a young child, and I snorted beer down my nose trying not to laugh. That broke any tension there had been, and talk moved on to more welcome subjects.

Alan was a natural storyteller, and kept me amused all afternoon with tales from the island. As an estate agent he got to meet a lot of people, and hear a lot of stories, most of them funny, some of them sad, and others very lewd indeed. We hardly noticed we were getting through rather a lot of beer until I went to the fridge and found it empty. As the sun set, chill air blew in, driving us indoors, and ending the first part of what was turning into quite a session.

We started on the Talisker while Alan cooked up some more fish—with mash potatoes this time—"for ballast," he said. We ate in the dining room, and as we were going back through to the sitting area, Alan looked at Beth's urn on the mantle.

He turned serious again.

"I see what you mean about the cottage not bothering you," he said quietly. "You've got something even closer to home on your mind, haven't you?"

Back in London, nobody would ever have asked such a direct question, but up here on the island, it didn't feel intrusive at all, just a natural extension of the other stories I'd been told that day. I said something vague about needing to have Beth close by me. Alan didn't push it; if he had, I might have started talking and not have been able to talk. He launched into a ribald story about a local vicar, two Swedish tourists and an incident in a phone booth.

Then we really started drinking.

The morning hangover was as epic as the drinking had been the night before.

I woke to the sound of clinking glass and got out of bed to investigate. Alan was already up and about, cleaning up the wreckage we'd left for the morning—beer bottles and glasses, two empty whisky bottles, plates still containing bits of our meal, and half-finished packets of salted peanuts and cheesy snacks. And above everything else, the place smelled of stale beer, Scotch and fish.

I left Alan at the sink and opened the French windows to their widest extent, letting the wind off the loch blow away my cobwebs. I took one look at the crofter's cottage, and realized I'd made a decision at some point during the night.

"Can I have it taken down?" I said to Alan once the chores were done and we were once more out on the patio—black coffee, and plenty of it this time. I pointed at the cottage. "It's blocking the view a bit and needs to go."

"You can do anything you like with it," he said. "It's yours."

"In that case, fuck it. I want it gone—every stone. Do you know somebody who'd do the job?"

"You should throw a party," he replied, smiling. "Half the island would come to cheer you on. But yes, I know just the man for the job. I'll get him to give you a ring."

"He's not scared of ghosts, is he?"

"Of course he is—he's an islander. But money trumps fear up here, every time."

We sat for a while just enjoying the morning.

"So is there anything else I should know before you go?"

He smiled, then groaned.

"Well, I've got a sore head, but then again, that makes two of us. No, the old lady was the main thing. There are other stories, of course, with a house this old. But that's all they are—stories. I doubt there ever was a Spaniard within several hundred miles of the place in the armada days, and as I've said, you can't swing a cat up here without hitting some spook or another. As long as you don't get the heebie-jeebies out here on your lonesome, you'll be fine."

We finished off three cups of coffee each before he pronounced himself fit to drive.

"I'll leave the dinghy here for a bit if you'd like?" he said. "There's a wee seal colony down the loch that's worth a visit, and some caves farther up the coast you can get inside. If you're looking for inspiration for a painting?"

"As long as we keep off the Scotch next time," I replied.

"Och, man—where would the fun be in that?"

He left with a promise to get a contractor to give me a quote for taking down the cottage, and I went back to bed.

7

The demolition of the crofter's cottage took less than an afternoon. I accepted a phone quote from the contractor the day after Alan's visit, and two days later the building was gone, thanks to the use of a small bulldozer and a chunky flatbed truck.

I watched proceedings from the patio. The two workmen were both fast and skillful, and the cottage was little more than a pile of rubble before I finished my coffee. What was left of the roof was lifted onto the truck in almost a single piece. After that it was just a matter of them getting all the loose stone into the back, a job that took less than an hour. I was amused to see the stoat poke his head out to see what all the rumpus was about before fleeing for the duration.

The older of the men accepted my offer of a beer when they were done. The younger declined and drove the truck away, heading off down the rutted track at a slow walking pace.

"There's a bit of a hole down there now, sir," the man said. "Some kind of root cellar by the looks of things. I wouldn't go wandering around along the shore in the dark. If you fell in and hurt yourself, it might be while afore anybody noticed."

"I don't intend to do much wandering," I said, laughing. "The view's just fine from here."

"I've lived in Dunvegan all my life, you know," he said. "But this is only the second time I've been out here."

I hesitated to ask, but the cottage was gone, it was a gorgeous day, and we had beer—what harm could a simple question do?

"When was the last time?" I asked.

I saw a similar hesitation in the man before he answered.

"It was the day before the old lady died," he said. "Funnily enough, she asked me to come and give her an estimate to take away the cottage. I gave her the same figure I gave you, and was waiting for a reply when I heard she was dead."

A sudden breeze came of the loch, a chill reminder of how quickly the weather could change. I felt it in my spine and shivered.

"Somebody walk over your grave?" the man asked.

I didn't answer, but the day no longer felt as gorgeous as before. He finished his beer and looked out over the loch.

"Your view is improved. I knew it would be," he said.

He was right about that. I now had a clear outlook right across the expanse of the loch to the hills on the far side. The only thing now between the patio and the shore was the woodpile. I hadn't had to use any of it yet, but I was looking forward to the winter when I could get a real fire going. I wasn't sure the stoat would enjoy being disturbed too often though, as he seemed to have taken up residence in and around the logs, and could be seen most mornings sunning himself before starting his day's foraging.

My own mood improved greatly in the weeks following the removal of the cottage. I got used to the solitude, and even started in on a new painting—a panoramic view from the patio. The dinghy still lay in the harbor below the kitchen, but I didn't have the confidence to take it out on my own. Alan was away working on the sale of a large estate north of Inverness for several weeks, and our next fishing trip was put off until his return.

I developed a liking for two things—mackerel pate and Talisker, sometimes both at the same time. The other item of note was that I had taken to talking to Beth as if she were in the room with me, mostly when I was working on the painting. My coffee rituals now also involved feeding not two, but six sparrows, the family having grown since my arrival. The stoat never came closer than the woodpile, but he watched me constantly, as did the seals just offshore.

Every Friday I went down to the village to get my provisions and stock up on booze, and on Saturday nights I walked down to the Dunvegan Arms, usually leaving again when the cabaret or band started up around nine, and being home by ten.

That was my routine through most of the summer.

The idyll was not to last.

I got the next corrupted email in the middle of August. As before, only two words stood out.

Stay down.

I took precautions against a malware attack, cleared up the laptop registry, deleted the cache and cookies, and ran three different virus scans. I woke the next morning to find a long streak of soot on the bathroom mirror and three more garbled emails.

A lesser man—or a more sane man—might have upped sticks and left at that point, but I'd grown fond of my new home, far too fond to be driven out by dirty streaks and badly spelled emails.

My war of attrition began in earnest that same weekend.

It started slowly.

Each morning I'd find a single streak of soot, somewhere in the house. Sometimes it would be partly hidden behind a curtain or almost behind the cooker, sometimes I would find it in plain sight on my laptop screen or the bathroom mirror. Each time I wiped the dirt away, muttered "fuck off" under my breath, and went about my business. I received a garbled email every second day or so, and after a few weeks of this I took to deleting them without even reading them.

I incorporated the morning check for soot and email into my daily routine, after shower and before coffee. That way I got to relax out on the patio and I could still feel as if the day was only just beginning. I refused to think of the irritations as any kind of supernatural visitations, preferring to consider them just a minor quirk of the house to be endured; a mental subterfuge, I know, but one I found surprisingly easy to maintain as the weeks went on.

I certainly fooled Alan. We had two more fishing trips with accompanying whisky-drinking sessions, and subsequent hangovers, before the end of summer, and I managed to make my morning checks both times without him spotting anything amiss. And so it went for a while, almost like a game of cat and mouse, although I wasn't yet sure which I was meant to be. Summer came to an end and the autumn brought with it a changeover to biting winds and heavy rain. My morning coffee got moved indoors to the dining table where I'd mostly sit and watch the rain lash against the windows or the fog creeping up the loch. Most days the stoat peeked out of the woodpile and scurried away again, as if he too had to change his ritual with the changing season. The sparrows, only four now, seemed to admonish me, finding the ball of fat and seeds I hung up outside poor fare in comparison to the digestive biscuits I'd been feeding them in the sunshine. The loch was mostly too choppy for me to see any seals, but I imagined them out on the water, watching the house, wondering where I'd gone.

The others who would be wondering where I'd got to would be the folks at the Dunvegan Arms. September was too wet and windy for me to even consider a walk along the loch to the village bar. I could of course have phoned for a cab, but in truth I felt cozy and settled where I was. There was also a nagging feeling that if I left for too long, something else—whatever was leaving me the messages—might decide to take full residence, although that was a thought I would not fully admit to myself.

Tormentor

My relative well-being was completely shattered on a Saturday in early October.

I woke, lying on my back, staring at the ceiling that had gained a six-inch streak of soot overnight, just off center about two feet from the light socket. I had to stand on the bed to reach it, and it was only when I was up close to the surface that I saw, under the old lining paper that had been painted over, the faint outline denoting there was a hatchway underneath.

Neither Alan, nor any of the particulars I'd had read about the house, had mentioned an attic, and I knew just from the dimensions and slope of the roof that any space up there was going to be small and cramped. But now that I knew about it, I had to look.

It took half an hour of cursing to tear the paper off the ceiling—and it was going to take twice as long to clear up the mess I made in doing so—but finally I had the hatchway cleared. It took almost all of my strength to force it open, and when I did, I got a blast of dust in my face that almost choked me. I spluttered and spat, and reached up into the open space. I was able to pull myself up easily enough and sat on the edge of the hatch, legs dangling down into the room below. A small skylight I hadn't even noticed from the outside let in enough light to see by.

The space was, as I had expected, cramped. My head brushed the main beam running the length of the house, and there was hardly enough room to crawl, even if I had wanted to.

It was also empty—or almost so. The only thing in view apart from undisturbed sawdust and motes dancing in the light from the window was a yellowed notebook. A dust-free hollow between it and the hatch made me think it had been hidden here to keep it away from prying eyes, pushed inside by someone standing on a bed below.

I took the notebook with me when I left the cramped space. I closed the hatch and, leaving the mess for later, showered, shaved and made some coffee. I only got round to looking at the book when I was once more sitting in the dining room. It looked to be a fine, clear morning on the loch, but I was more interested in what I had found than the view.

It was a lined workbook, the kind I remember from my own schooldays. The cover was yellowed and faded but the lion rampant on the front was still clearly visible despite a growth of slime or mold on the surface. Above the lion was written, in a heavy, childish hand and gone over two or three times for impact, *Annie's Diary, August 1955.*

When I opened it, the writing was clearly legible, and the first sentence ensured I was gripped from the start.

Monday 3rd—Something got into the barn and spooked the cows last night. I woke up in the dark and heard them, bellowing as if they were being slaughtered. Dad said it must have been a fox, as there's nothing else round here that would set them off like that. Whatever it was, it ruined the milk too, which was thin and gray and looked like it had soot in it. Dad was not a bit pleased. He was told when we took this place that the grass around here was perfect for milkers. We've hardly had a decent gallon since we got here.

Not like back at the old farm. We had foxes there too, and squirrels and all sorts of beasties in and out of the barn day and night, but we never had any problem with the milk. I wish we were back there now.

I miss Kinross. The school in Dunvegan is going to be nice enough, but it's a month yet before I start, and all my friends are far away. It seems like a long time since I had anyone to talk to. Mum says I'll get used to it, but there's something not right here. Maybe it's because I'm alone most of the time, but I was alone a lot back at the farm, so that's not it. Old Man Thomas who has the small cottage on the shore says I'm away with the fey folk, but I'm too old now to believe that nonsense.

Tormentor

Maybe keeping this diary will help me with the boredom. In any case, I've decided it will at least make the long nights pass faster—at least until next year when I can get out of here to the big school in Oban. I aim to write something every day, although I can't say as there will ever be much to write about.

Tuesday 4th—*Bored. It's raining outside, and it's too cold. I thought August was supposed to be summertime? Well it's not around here. Dad's been muttering about the milk being bad again, and Mum's too busy cleaning the house to talk to me. Bored.*

Wednesday 5th—*Got told off by Mum for trailing dirt into the house. It wasn't me! She showed me the mark, just by the kitchen door—long, black and streaky. I told her it looked like something Old Man Thomas would do, for I've seen him drawing his matchstick men on the walls down in the crofter's cottage, but Mum was having none of it. She told me I should be ashamed of myself for trying to blame a poor old man. I've been sent to bed early. It's just not fair.*

Thursday 6th—*There's been more dirty marks in the house—lots of them. Mum's really angry, and Dad and I don't know what we can do. We've told her over and over again that it's not us that's doing it, but she just keeps shouting. She's been crying too, although she got angry again when Dad mentioned it. He's gone out to the barn for a bit to see to the cows and things are quiet—for now.*

It didn't help that Old Man Thomas laughed like a madman when I told him about the soot. He says the fey folk have found their way into the house, and that's the end of it. We'll never be rid of them now.

Friday 7th—*Mum and Dad are having a huge argument—I can hear them through the walls. Mum got all weepy today and told Dad she wanted to go back to Kinross. Dad says that's impossible, even if we wanted to, as there's no money to pay for a move. Mum said she'll take me and go and stay with Gran in Cupar, and Dad started shouting, and now they're both at it.*

43

I think it's got to do with the soot marks — they're driving Mum mad. I'm sure Old Man Thomas is doing it, so I'm going to sit up tonight and watch at the window. I'll catch him, and Mum and Dad will stop shouting at each other, and everything will go back to normal.

Saturday 8th *— I fell asleep. I tried to stay up, but I just got too tired. More soot marks this morning. Mum and Dad aren't talking, and Old Man Thomas just laughs. I went out to the cows to get away for a bit, but the milk is spoiled again, and when I told Dad he had a face like thunder. He went down to Old Man Thomas' cottage and I heard him shouting and cursing at the old man to stop playing silly beggars. I hope that's the end of it.*

Sunday 9th *— Disaster. We all went to church this morning. Old Man Thomas stayed behind as usual. We saw the smoke from all the way down in Dunvegan, and although Dad got the post office man to get the van out and get us back here right quick, we were too late to save the barn. The poor cows — all burned away.*

Monday 10th *— Dad called the bobbies to talk to the old man. He's sure it was him that lit the fire in the barn, but they went away again and Old Man Thomas is still out there laughing and cackling. I walked down to the shore earlier and looked in his door. He's got the wall covered now with his wee stick men, all black and thin and nasty looking. I don't like them. I don't like them one bit.*

Tuesday 11th *— We're going home! Well, to Gran's anyway. I'll leave this diary here in case we come back, but with the old man killing himself like that just next door, I can't see Mum wanting to have anything to do with the place ever again. Hurrah!*

8

That was it—the rest of the notebook was just slightly damp, empty pages. There was no clue as to what had finally driven them away, but I guessed it was the old man dying in the cottage on the shore. And I had a pretty good idea of how he'd gone—I could almost see the flames in my mind. My decision to raze the old ruin to the ground was feeling more right by the minute.

The girl's diary left more questions than answers—of course it did—but in my mind it was all tied to the old cottage, and I'd already got rid of that. So what if I kept getting soot marks? That's all they were, marks, and they weren't doing me any harm.

I had a sentimental moment while cleaning up the mess in my room, and put the notebook back where I had found it. It was obvious the girl wasn't going to come back for it, but somehow it just felt right.

It took most of the morning to clear up the flaked paint, tattered paper and dust I'd dislodged in my attempt to get to the attic. There was a bare patch on the ceiling now that I was going to have to look at until I got into Portree to buy some paint and brushes, but that couldn't be helped.

I went through and opened the patio doors wide despite the chill outside, and stood there for a while, letting my mind drift, letting the quiet fill me and drive out any thoughts of burning barns and matchstick men.

That afternoon I put my landscape painting away. The light wasn't going to be right again for it until next summer anyway. I started on something new, an abstract that was a style completely new for me, but one I could see clear as day in my mind's eye. It was going to work well, if I could only transfer it onto paper. I was so lost in it I jumped several inches when my phone rang. As it happens, I was working on a dark area, and I left a thin black streak, six inches long, on the canvas.

The call was a wrong number, but when I went back to the painting, my enthusiasm for the task had drained away, so I left it where I'd stopped, black streak and all.

I looked out the window to see clear blue sky. It being Saturday, I decided it was well past time I had a few beers down in Dunvegan. I put on a heavy jacket and my walking boots, placed the flashlight in the deep inside pocket, and headed down the shore.

———

Tourist season was long finished. Dunvegan Castle sat, squat, solid and quiet on its rocky promontory with only the mildest of lapping waves and the squawk of gulls high above to disturb it. The girl's diary and its talk of the fey folk reminded me of the castle's most famous exhibit—the Am Bratach Sìth, the Fairy Flag of the MacLeods. I knew there were many legends associated with the ancestral heirloom, and wondered if any of them were linked to my house. After all, it was the nearest dwelling to the northeast of the old castle.

As I got settled in the Dunvegan Arms twenty minutes later, I started my attempt to steer the conversation toward the subject, knowing it might take all night. Indeed we might never get round to it.

The locals were in talkative moods—old George in particular. George was probably the oldest man in town, certainly the oldest still active enough to get out to the bar for an evening.

"I was glad to see you got rid of the cottage," were his opening words to me as I joined him and his cronies at their corner table.

Tormentor

"At least I've improved the view," I replied, a noncommittal gambit to start with.

"Improved more than that, I'd bet," Sandy Johnston added. Sandy was George's straight man, and together they made a double act that kept the bar entertained for hours at a time.

Over the evening I learned many things. Farmer Donnie Fraser lost his whole potato crop that year to a blight; the back road was shut again due to "bloody council incompetence." It had been a good year for tourism in the town, and still nobody was going to tell me anything about my house or its history. It seems my inclusion into their ranks only went so far. The company was good though, and I thoroughly enjoyed all their stories and banter. I had a most pleasant evening, and even considered staying past my normal leaving time, but as soon as the band started up at nine—a Sixties tribute band, badly out of tune and with voices like strangled cats—I made my excuses and went out into the night.

Fog had rolled in—candy-floss thick and wet against my cheeks, with visibility ten yards and less. I wasn't too worried as I knew the track well and had my flashlight.

The early part of my walk home went smoothly enough as I climbed the small hill out of town and up the avenue past the castle car park. I almost shit myself when a large owl swooped down from the trees and passed over my head while checking out this interloper in its territory but that was the only movement I saw for the next half hour, lost in a moving wall of gray dampness.

Things got worse when I strayed off the path—I know, I know, I've seen all those movies, too. Keep to the path, beware of the moors. Luckily on this particular track it wasn't possible to stray far without meeting the sea on one side and gorse or bog too impenetrable to pass on the other. I was able to find the track again after a diversion in a particularly soggy patch, but not before getting soaked up to the knees and tearing several long rips in my favorite trousers.

I was uncomfortably damp and thoroughly fed up as I approached where I knew the house to be. The trouble was the fog was even thicker now and although I must have been within ten yards of my own home, I couldn't find the bloody thing at first. I stood still, pointed the flashlight at the ground, and turned full circle. Something caught my eye—a darker patch.

The woodpile?

I walked over and shone the light in that direction. I stood over the space where the old crofter's cottage had been. As the contractor said, there was indeed a hole belowground. The flashlight showed a six-foot or so cube, mostly lying in deep shadow. The floor looked like packed earth, and there was no sign that anything had been stored there for a very long time. I crouched on my haunches and shone the light on the walls.

Two minutes later I was standing with my back to the French windows of my house with no memory of how I'd got there. My mind was full of what I revealed on the walls of the cellar—black lines, matchstick figures, hundreds of them, dancing and cavorting in the unsteady beam of my flashlight.

The next morning I found a sooty streak down my bathroom mirror, and that was it—my rationality only stretched so far, I'd had enough. As I've said before, my natural tendency is to run. I decided it had better be sooner rather than later.

I didn't even bother to clean off the streak. I went straight to the phone, intending to call Alan and tell him to get the property listed for sale, never mind it was early Sunday morning and he'd more than likely be nursing a hangover. The laptop pinged at me as I picked up the phone. I had three emails, garbled English again, and with only several words clearly standing out.

They were different words this time.

Stay. Beth needs you.

9

Now I wanted to run even farther, but as I stood and turned away from the laptop, I looked straight at the urn on the mantel.

What if?

So I stayed. I wiped clean the bathroom mirror and stuck to my routine. I took my morning coffee out onto the patio. The fog had lifted, leaving a crisp, clear morning with more than a hint of the winter chills to come. The stoat seemed bemused to see me again, and sat on top of the woodpile, head tilted to one side, staring at me as if I could be hypnotized like a frightened rabbit. Three sparrows trotted around near my feet, but I had no crumbs of comfort for them that morning.

My gaze kept being drawn to the hole I'd looked down into the night before. I'd backed away from it so quickly I only had the vaguest of memories of what I had seen beyond the stick figures. I'd let the dancing beam of light from my flashlight spook me in the fog and the dark. But now it was the cold light of day. I decided to take another look.

I fetched my phone from the desk and went back outside.

Part of me—a larger part than I was willing to admit—believed that I'd find only blank walls, that I'd had a mental fog as thick as the real one I'd been lost in, and imagined the whole thing. I was almost surprised when I crouched down and saw the black lines scrawled on every available surface. I used the camera in the phone to take as many pictures as I could. To do the job properly would have involved dropping down into the cellar and taking a series of photographs that could be spliced into a panorama, but I wasn't at all sure I'd be able to pull myself back out, so did what I was able to do from above.

I took the phone inside, transferred the pictures onto the laptop, and tried to make sense of what I was looking at. Whoever had drawn the figures had packed them tightly, a miniature army ranked side by side in tightly regimented formation. Some had all four limbs, some were missing an arm or a leg, and some were just a single streak with a dot for the head, like an upside-down exclamation mark. It did not take long to realize that I was not actually looking at matchstick men at all. It was a code, maybe even a language, just one with which I was completely unfamiliar.

I spent the rest of the day online, which proved to be both expensive and fruitless. I couldn't find any analogous scripts anywhere. I posted my pictures in several linguistics forums, hoping that someone might have an idea what I'd stumbled upon, but by the time I logged off in late afternoon, I'd not had any replies.

There were no further emails either.

I had my afternoon snack sitting in the dining room, facing, not out to the view, but up at the mantel, to Beth's urn. I'd always believed that the contents were all that was left of her. Most of her had been scattered to the winds that day in the crematorium and the urn itself was my link to better days in the past, not the future.

Beth hadn't been a believer either. She wanted to dance in the cosmos, to be scattered far and wide, ashes to ashes, stardust to stardust. I'd complied with those wishes. I had no expectation of ever being with her again in some mythical better place. My consolation was in the thought that bits of me, and bits of her, however small, would mingle and coexist throughout eternity—maybe not conscious, but existing nonetheless.

Tormentor

Now I found I needed to adjust my reality paradigm, and my mind had trouble with it. I could no longer explain away the soot marks as a quirk of the house—something was at work here. It might be some way outside my view of how things were supposed to work, but just as I'd been reminded the night before, people in the movies spend too much time questioning what is immediately obvious to anybody who has seen a few films. I resolved not to go down that route. Something was trying to communicate with me. I had a duty—to both myself and to Beth, to try to talk back.

I started with my pictures of the stick figures. I wasn't particularly keen on puzzles, but I'd spent plenty of time as a computer programmer and knew how to both build things up, and break them down into simple principal components. I approached the pictographs as I would approach a piece of code that needed to be analyzed.

It became obvious that the figures were arranged in clusters—groups of eight that immediately had me thinking of bits and bytes and wondering if it was indeed a representation of a computer program. But no matter which way I tried to splice my pictures together, I could not find a starting, or indeed an ending, point, and could not make sense of what had been represented. My notes looked like something from a war-zone surgery.

Left arm gone, right leg gone, all limbs intact, no head, legs gone, no arms, limbs intact, left leg and left arm gone.

Right arm gone, no head, no legs, no arms, no limbs, right leg gone, all limbs intact, left leg gone.

I drew out grids of eight, over and over again, looking for a pattern. I found one repeater, a group that came up at regular intervals across all my pictures.

No limbs, no limbs, no head, no head, left arm gone, left leg gone, no legs, no head.

51

For a time—a short time—I thought I might be getting somewhere, but that was the extent of my discovery. I was surprised to look up and see it was near midnight, but not at all surprised to be almost immediately hit with a pounding headache bought on by peering at the stick figures all evening.

I lay in bed for hours, staring at the hatchway in the ceiling, watching the play of shadow through the room, and wondering whether I had joined the previous inhabitants of the house in going ever so slightly insane.

The next morning I found the expected soot smudge on my laptop screen, but this time it was more than a single stroke; there was a dot above it—a head. I had an epiphany, and drew a grid, eight by eight. In the first box, top left, I drew a stick figure, just a body and head.

My morning routine from then on included drawing the day's smudge in its place on the grid. After eight days I had my first group—the repeater.

No limbs, no limbs, no head, no head, left arm gone, left leg gone, no legs, no head.

I was definitely getting somewhere.

10

Alan arrived on the middle Saturday in October to get the dinghy out of the water before the weather got too bad. It happened to be a clear, calm day with barely a ripple on the surface of the loch.

"What do you say?" he said. "A wee trip down the loch, then a few beers in the Dunvegan later? That is if you don't mind me kipping on your couch again?"

"Just as long as you still respect me in the morning," I said.

Truthfully, I was happy for the company. I'd spent most of the week trying to solve the riddle of the pictograms until it felt like I was bashing my head against a brick wall. A trip on the water and a few—maybe more than a few—beers sounded like perfect medicine to me.

Alan was also more voluble than the regulars in the Dunvegan Arms. On our trip down the loch he kept me entertained with a potted history of the MacLeod clan and the old castle. I didn't even have to mention the famous Fairy Flag—he gave me chapter and verse on all the various myths and legends, of which there are many. I couldn't see any correlation with my own circumstances, until a single sentence knocked me for a loop.

"The flag used to be covered in writing, or so they say," Alan said. "Or rather drawings—little black lines and crosses. They're all faded now, but nobody could ever figure out what they were anyway and..."

I'd tuned him out. Little black lines and crosses. I was afraid I knew exactly what those might have been.

We were in the bay to the immediate north of the castle.

"Is it open?" I asked, interrupting him.

"The castle? No. They bugger off to warmer climes after the end of September. Can't say as I blame them. They open up again around Easter."

It looked like I wasn't going to get any help from that quarter. But now that I knew, I would be able to do some digging online. There might be some old photographs of the flag, something that might even help me with the pictographs.

"Are you okay?" Alan asked. "You've gone awful quiet."

I almost told him, but bit my tongue. I'd have to tell him it all if I started—about the soot smudges and the crofter's cottage, and if I did, I feared he'd think I was suffering from similar delusions to the previous occupant. So I held my peace.

"Just a bit of a headache. Nothing a few beers won't cure," I replied.

"I thought you'd never ask," he said.

We went back up the loch at speed—quite exhilarating in the small dinghy. It took us ten minutes to get it out of the water and up onto the trailer. I went to fetch the flashlight.

"What do you need that for?" Alan asked.

"The walk back," I replied.

"Walk? Me? I think not. We'll get a taxi."

While he was on his phone, I sneaked in a quick image search for the old flag. I found what I was looking for almost immediately. The photograph was dated 1912, and there they were, painted onto the thin silk—matchstick figures, eight of them. I recognized the pattern straightaway. It was the repeater.

No limbs, no limbs, no head, no head, left arm gone, left leg gone, no legs, no head.

Alan fit right in at the Dunvegan Arms, being well-known to most of the locals.

"Where's your dad?" old George asked. "The auld bugger owes me a fiver."

"Can I pay you in dancing girls?" Alan replied, and George laughed.

"That reminds me of a time in 'Frisco back in sixty-five when..."

And away we went, on a night of stories and booze, more stories and more booze. The band started up at nine, but I didn't go home, although the noise did drive me out into the street for some respite after half an hour or so. Old George came out and joined me, lighting up a smoke.

"Are you okay, son?" he asked.

That was the second time today I'd been asked that. Maybe I wasn't doing as well as I thought, or maybe I'd just spent too long mulling over the pictograms.

"Just been working on some stuff," I replied.

The old man took a long draw of smoke before replying.

"You need to get out and about among people more often," he said. "It doesn't do to lock yourself away—especially after losing your wife. Trust me, son, I know. I've been there myself."

I could see it in his eyes—the same grief that had eaten away at me for the two years after Beth passed. But I wasn't grieving now, hadn't been for some time. How could I explain that to an old man who obviously only wanted to help? The simple answer is that I couldn't. I muttered something about getting down to the pub more often, he finished his smoke and clapped me on the back as we went inside. And that was the end of his attempt to buck up my ideas. Perhaps I really should have listened to him.

The night rolled on—Alan proved himself a trouper during an extended karaoke session that saw him doing fine impressions of Elton John, Elvis and Mick Jagger, and I drank more Scotch than was good for me before we were finally bundled into the taxi somewhere around one o' clock.

I was in bed and asleep, fully clothed, by quarter past.

I woke, disoriented in the dark, wondering why I was still dressed and on top of the covers, then more worried that my head might fall off as the effects of the booze made themselves felt. My bladder called for release and I managed to get up—half rolling off the bed to stagger to the bathroom. I only put on the small light above the mirror so as not to disturb Alan who lay sprawled on the couch snoring like thunder. After flushing, I turned to the washbasin, just in time to see a black streak form on the mirror, appearing from nowhere.

"Beth," I whispered. "Is that you?"

A dot was added above the original line, as if to punctuate my question.

"Beth?"

Another single stroke added a left leg to the figure.

"For pity's sake—tell me what I should do."

There was no further answer. I stood and stared at the figure for several seconds, then my brain remembered I was still drunk and drove me, staggering and bumping into furniture, back to my room, where I tried and failed to get my trousers off and fell back onto the bed.

The rest is darkness.

When I finally surfaced, thin sunlight was coming in the window. I heard the toilet flush, then Alan opening and closing cupboards in the kitchen area as the kettle began to whistle. I dragged myself out to meet the day.

I felt moderately better after a shower, and by the time we went out onto the patio with some toast and coffee I was almost human.

"I cleaned the bathroom mirror," Alan said, giving me a jolt.

"Shit—I forgot about that."

I went back inside to my desk and added the latest stick figure to my grid. Alan stood at the French doors looking at me.

"I saw that earlier, too. Want to tell me what's going on?"

"Not really," I replied, and went back out to the patio.

"Wee black lines and crosses? Come on, I'm not stupid. This is Mrs. Menzies all over again, only you've got it conflated somehow with the auld flag and the fairies. This isn't healthy."

I sat and looked over the view—my view. There was no sign of the stoat, or the sparrows, and suddenly all I wanted was solitude, quiet, and more time to study the pictographs.

"It's all I've got, Alan," I said softly. "I came here because I was in need... I didn't know what I needed. But I do now. This place is good for me."

He didn't look convinced.

"Just promise me you'll call if it gets too much for you, or even if you just fancy a beer. You should come over to Portree, see the bright lights and the big city."

I managed a laugh.

"What—the chippie and the George Hotel bar again?"

He didn't rise to the bait—that's when I knew he was serious.

"I don't want to have to try to sell this place again," he said. "Look where it got me the last time—drunk and hungover on a strange man's couch on a Sunday morning."

"Hey, I'm not a strange man."

"Well, that's a matter of opinion."

I thought we'd steered the conversation away from the pictograms, but I was wrong.

"I'll tell you my theory about the wee scribbles—if you're interested?" he said.

"Oh, I'm interested all right. I've been trying to find a starting point for weeks now. I'll fetch more coffee and you can fill me in."

When I came back with a fresh pot, he had the page with my grid layout in his hand.

"I used to know a drummer, back at uni," he said, and tapped the paper. "And when he was practicing, he worked from sheets that looked remarkably similar to this. I think what you have here isn't a code—or rather, it is, but not in words. It's some kind of rhythm."

It was another moment of epiphany.

"And a flag that was being carried into battle might have a drumbeat imprinted on it—one that could easily be seen, and followed?"

I took the sheet of paper from him and ran a finger along the repeater line.

No limbs, no limbs, no head, no head, left arm gone, left leg gone, no legs, no head.

"But we still don't know what the individual figures indicate. Long beats, short beats, double beats—it could be anything. And we don't know why they're turning up here, in the house."

Alan looked like he might say something in reply, but took a long sip of coffee and looked at me over the top of the cup, as if assessing my mental health.

"I never said it was a good theory," he finally replied.

"No, but I think you're on to something. I'll look into it later."

"Hey, I don't want to be blamed for sending you off the rails completely," he said. "Promise me you'll take it easy."

I scarcely heard him—I was already studying the pictograms, looking for a key to unlock the rhythm.

———————

I was still at it when Alan left ten minutes later.

"Remember—you promised," he said as he left.

Actually I had done no such thing, and within minutes of the SUV driving off down the track I was back at it.

For the rest of the morning I sat out on the patio, drinking too much coffee, my head pounding in a rhythm of its own. The chill did a lot to help the hangover pass, and I was cheered when the stoat felt comfortable enough to sneak out and watch me from the woodpile. The sparrows returned soon after that, and made short work of the remains of the toast. When a seal barked just off shore, I felt quiet seep into me; I relaxed for the first time since getting up.

A colder wind came with the turning of the tide, finally driving me indoors in early afternoon.

I had new email. Most of the text was garbled as before, but at the very bottom was a string of numbers, and I knew immediately what they meant.

1,1,2,2,3,5,9,2

I'd been given the rhythm signature of the repeater line.

No limbs, no limbs, no head, no head, left arm gone, left leg gone, no legs, no head.

It wasn't enough for me to decode all the pictograms—not yet. But it gave me a start.

I spent the rest of that day writing code. I reproduced the pictograms in my grid into beeps at the appropriate rhythm, filling in the missing beats with best guesses where I could in a cyclical loop that would play through all possible permutations. It didn't take me long. I left it to play softly in the background as I continued to work on decoding the parts where I'd had to improvise.

I soon got used to the beeping—indeed it was almost soothing. I found it so calming that I left it on in the main room when I went to bed; the beeps played a lullaby as I drifted off into darkness where Beth waited for me, smiling.

11

I spent ten minutes looking for the soot mark in the morning. There wasn't one, but I had more email. At the foot of a garbled text message was an eight-by-thirty grid of numbers, the repeater showing up every six lines or so, with all the numbers I had only guessed at filled in.

I had my complete message. I just didn't quite know what to do with it.

I coded the grid into the program I'd written the day before and set it to play in the background on the laptop. The beat accompanied me all day, most of which was spent sitting either on the patio, or on the sofa, in anticipation of an outcome.

There was none forthcoming—not that day, or the next, although yet again there was no smudge mark in the morning. I felt vaguely disappointed, as if I'd been handed a message and told to pass it on with being given any idea what it contained, and without any thanks.

I developed a slight obsession with checking my inbox, hoping for another clue, something to tell me things were still moving on toward some kind of a conclusion. Apart from a couple of invitations to Christmas parties in London, I got nothing.

I kept playing the rhythmic beeps for the rest of the week but got no reply. There was no recurrence of the soot marks, no more email. The following Saturday I switched off the laptop when I went to the pub. There was no soot mark on Sunday, so I left it off.

It seemed my foray into the Twilight Zone was over before it had really begun.

PART 2: DOORWAY

1

I settled back into a new routine — I redecorated my bedroom ceiling, got the root cellar filled in with stones and gravel from the shore, painted in the mornings and watched movies at night. On Saturdays I took a taxi down and back to the Dunvegan Arms. My coffee ritual changed from sitting out on the patio to standing by the open door; the stoat still kept an eye on me, and three sparrows were well fed through the rest of October and into November.

There were no more soot marks, no more garbled emails, and part of me felt like I had lost Beth all over again. I drank more than I should, both down at the pub and in the comfort of my own home, and I often switched on the rhythmic beeps on the laptop, just in case.

In mid-November I braved the elements, drove across the island and took Alan up on his offer of a night out in Portree. We had a great time, although I'm afraid to say it got hazy later on in the evening. I do remember joining him on karaoke for a very drunken rendition of some Rolling Stones songs, but beyond that the night is mostly an alcohol-induced blur.

The hangover was equally epic on the Sunday morning.

"What are you doing for Christmas?" Alan asked over coffee in his flat overlooking the old harbor.

"Sobering up," I replied, and groaned as he pushed a plate laden with fried eggs, bacon, sausages, baked beans and toast in front of me.

"Breakfast of champions," he said. "Get it down you."

"I thought that was sex?" I replied.

"This is better for you," he said, and took to his own breakfast with gusto. Once I started eating, I was surprised to find myself enjoying the meal, despite the hangover.

We polished the food off in short order.

"So, Christmas?" he asked again. "Any plans?"

"I've got a couple of invitations to go back down south..." I started before he waved me to quiet.

"And miss your first island festivities? Oh no. That won't do. That won't do at all. You can come round to Mum and Dad's place in the afternoon. She'll do us all proud, we can eat and drink until we're pished and stuffed, and fall asleep in front of a Bond movie. Then in the evening, there's a dance in the George. It's always a great do—if we're lucky, we might even get a fight. Come on, you'll love it."

In truth I really wasn't keen on traveling the length of the country before and after the holiday season, and seeing old friends would only remind me of being with them when Beth was around. A new experience, with new friends, sounded like the perfect tonic.

"Okay, you've twisted my arm."

"Excellent. I'll go and kill a boar for roasting. Let the feasting begin."

We had another coffee after breakfast, sitting out on the quayside on the harbor before I declared myself sober enough to drive home.

"Hold on, I nearly forgot," Alan said, and dashed back indoors. He came out and handed me a small book. It looked to be a children's issue, and of some age judging by the faded and torn cover. The title was clear enough—*Folk Tales of the Isles*.

"I was telling Dad about your wee crosses and squiggles," he said. "And when I mentioned my drummer pal, he remembered this. You want page fifty-four."

I flipped to the required page. The story was titled "The Dunvegan Drummer Boy." Suddenly I'd have given anything to be back in London, with Beth and old pals, sinking a few glasses of wine and with nothing more to worry about than which restaurant to visit that evening.

Alan must have seen something in my eyes.

"Give it back," he said. "It was a bad idea. Sorry."

I pulled the book away from him. "No, you're okay. I'll take it. It's just a bit of a shock, that's all. I thought I was finished with all that stuff."

"Until daft me brings it all up again. Look, it's just a kids' story—and Dad says it's the only time he's ever heard of it, so it's not as if it's common knowledge or anything. It means nothing."

"Then it's okay if I read it, isn't it" I replied, managing a smile.

"Your superior logic defeats me again, Spock," he said, and gave me a smile in return.

"Remember, you're booked for Christmas," he said as I got into my car.

It was a glorious drive back across the island—clear blue skies, white horses in the bays and a touch of frost on the hilltops. I saw little of it. The book lay on the passenger seat beside me, and it called out to be read all the way back to the cottage.

2

The area around Dunvegan on Skye has long been known as one of the most haunted places in the islands, if not in the whole country.

Thanks for telling me.

That was the first line of the story, and it didn't get much more reassuring after that. I was sitting out on the patio—I had two wooly jumpers on, and my thick socks, and still I felt cold, but I was more comfortable reading this particular tale out in the open.

There are so many stories to be told it is hard to pick just one, but perhaps the strangest of all is the tale of the Drummer Boy of the MacLeods.

Donald's family were fisher folk, making a living off the bounty of Loch Dunvegan from a house of the eastern shore to the north of the castle, but Donald's eye was always being drawn to the castle itself, to the soldiers, and to fortune and glory. In his head he was a drummer boy, and he beat out martial rhythms on all available surfaces in the house, driving his mother to distraction by holding mock battles with plates, cutlery and anything else that came to hand as he led his army in the fray.

When the call came for the clans to join Bonnie Prince Charlie's rebellion, the chief called for all available men to join him. Donald's father was one of the first men to declare allegiance, but Donald was to be left to look after his mother and sisters. The boy would have none of it.

At the banquet before sailing, he sneaked in to the great hall with his bodhran in hand and even as the chief addressed the men, started up his beat. Donald's father was furious, and would have had the boy beaten to within an inch of his life, but even as he tried to snatch the drum from the boy, a cry went up in the crowd.

To a man they turned. The old flag was fluttering above them, although there was no breeze in the hall. And as they watched, strange markings appeared on the aged silk—black crosses and lines that coincided with the beats of Donald's wee drum.

The chief took this to be an omen.

"Where did the boy learn to do such a thing?" he asked.

Donald's father could not reply, and the boy himself did not say, although he smiled, somewhat sadly, even as the chief declared that he would be the one to lead the men in the coming battles.

The very next day they went off to war. There is no need to tell here of the bloody failure of the rebellion, although it is said that Donald never flinched from his duty through the long campaign, even when called to lead the final doomed march onto the field of Culloden.

It is said that Donald's mother knew the exact moment when the boy fell, so far away on the highland moor, for a drum beat out a rhythm that shook the whole house. Donald's father returned weeks later and they put the boy's body to final rest.

They buried the bodhran with him, and folks around Dunvegan swear that to this day, on quiet nights the boy

can still be heard in and around the house, beating the
drum and calling his army to battle.

I thought I had a bloody good idea exactly what house the story was referring to. The book was dated 1922, but the story, set as it was in Jacobite times, took the tale back to the mid-eighteenth century. And it seems I'd been wrong about the markings on the flag—they had come after the rhythm was set, and were not the source of it. Whatever it was I had uncovered over the summer and early autumn, it was far older than I had previously thought.

However, it all seemed moot now. There had been no soot marks for weeks, and no more anonymous email correspondence. I left the book on the mantel to remind myself to return it to Alan's father, and went back to my routine.

There was one more thing of note.

I developed a nervous habit. It started one early December morning out on the patio. I was feeding the sparrows when I caught myself drumming with the fingers of my left hand on the table. It took several seconds for me to realize it was the repeater beat. As my fingers moved, I saw the associated soot marks in my mind; *no limbs, no limbs, no head, no head, left arm gone, left leg gone, no legs, no head.*

Realizing what I was doing, I stopped at the third repeat, but at intervals in the days following I noticed it happening more often, especially if I let my mind drift. It wasn't too difficult to control, just bloody annoying, and I put it down to having spent so much time listening to the programmed beeps I'd set up on the laptop. To stop myself being tempted in the future, I deleted the program and burned my worksheet containing the grids. With a small degree of concentrating on what I was doing, I was also able to suppress the finger twitching completely, and I finally thought I was completely rid of the earlier compulsions that had gripped me.

In the second week of December I gave in to the growing chill in the house and started lighting a fire in the main grate. The stoat was not at all happy at me infringing on his domain when I went to fetch the first load of wood. He hissed at me angrily, but after that he seemed resigned to losing his perch and took to glaring at me from the dwindling pile each time I stocked up.

The sparrows weren't at all happy that I was spending less and less time with the patio doors open. They took to tapping on the window with their beaks in attempts to get my attention, and I usually gave in to their demands when my fingers threatened to tap along in time.

Having the fire going in the main room meant that my gaze was often focused on the fireplace itself, and on the mantel in particular. I took to talking to Beth again, especially while painting, and at times it felt like our conversations were guiding my brushstrokes. The abstract had become a dense, multilayered riot of color, predominately black and red but shot through with golden yellow and azure blue. I saw now it was not as abstract as I had thought, but was in fact a seascape, of sorts, but not of any view I had ever set eyes on.

3

On the Saturday before Christmas I took a taxi down to the Dunvegan Arms.

"You're looking well, son," was the first thing old George said as I joined the usual crowd in the snug. I ordered a round and it was only when I returned from the bar that I realized we had a new member of the Saturday Club—the local minister, Alexander Wark. I'd seen him around town, but never spoken. He'd always looked dour and forbidding, and was the last person I'd have expected to join the little group of drinkers I had come to call friends.

"Don't mind auld Alex here," George said, laughing. "He's not about to give us a lecture on the perils of drink. He likes to come in around Christmas for his one night of drunken debauchery a year."

The minister smiled and looked like a completely different man.

"Aye, on every other Saturday night I'm over at your place shagging your wife."

Once again we were off and running for a night of jokes, stories and not a little verbal abuse. Alex Wark proved more than capable of giving as good as he got; he was also a fount of scurrilous gossip that would have dismayed the ladies of the town had they heard it uttered, here in the local bar.

"And what about you, lad?" the minister asked, an hour or so and several beers into the evening. "How are the Spaniards treating you?"

You could have heard a pin drop. Everyone round the table went quiet, so much so that we could hear some of the local youths working up to a fight in the main bar.

Alex laughed and addressed the other men around the table.

"Come on, you mean you've let the lad live up in that house all this time and you haven't told him its history? Shame on you. That's no way to treat a pal."

"We didn't want to frighten him," Sandy Johnston said.

"Didn't want to frighten yourselves, you mean?" the minister replied. He turned to me.

"Get me a Talisker and I'll tell you a story," he said.

I didn't need to be asked a second time.

"How much do you know about the house?" he asked. We'd taken ourselves off to one side. Old George launched into one of his stories as the others studiously ignored us, which was fine by me.

I told Wark what I thought I knew—about Mrs. Menzies, about old Tom dying in the cottage fire, and about the wee drummer boy.

He laughed.

"My, you have been busy—and all that without even talking to these reprobates here about it. And what haven't you told me?" He put a hand out and covered my left fingers—they had started to twitch. "I've seen that before—Annie Menzies had the same affliction, not long before she passed."

I wasn't about to tell a man I'd only just met about the soot marks, or the messages on the laptop, or the beeps and rhythms of the message—that's how I now thought of it; a message I was never able to decipher. He seemed to see some of it in my eyes though.

"The house is getting to you, isn't it? You shouldn't let it. They're only stories—a strong man has nothing to fear from stories."

"And what about a weak man?" I said softly.

He smiled.

"That's what I'm here for," he said. "Any time you need to talk, you know where the church is."

65

"I'm not a believer."

"It's not compulsory," he said, and laughed. "But you didn't buy me a drink to get a sales pitch. You bought a story—another story."

He took a sip of the Talisker before continuing.

"You've probably realized by now that your house is old. You've gone back in your stories to the time of the rebellion, but it's older than that—much older. I suspect that some of the stonework might even go back to the earliest inhabited history of the island, several thousand years before Christ. Short of mounting a full-scale archaeological dig, the really early stuff is probably lost forever in the mists of time. But there is something I can tell you—the church has extensive records, as has the castle, and I pride myself on being something of a local historian. That's how I know that there is a basis in truth in the name of the house. There was indeed a Spaniard—or rather, several of them.

"The aftermath of their defeat by Drake saw many armada vessels attempt to make their escape by heading up the east coast and through the Pentland Firth to try to lose themselves in the islands before making south to home. Most didn't make it—the seas around northern Scotland are treacherous at the best of times, and that, combined with one of the worst storms in memory, meant that many Spaniards were dashed on Scotland's rocky shores. Five of them, in a single lifeboat, ended up here.

"Their names are written in the parish records if you choose to look—there is no denying they were here. Just as there is no denying they were given your house to stay in and work the land. It's written that it was a gift, of sorts, from the church—'Ye dwelling and five acres that no honest man will touch, for it be blighted.'"

I stopped him there.

"Why weren't they imprisoned? Weren't we at war with Spain?"

The minister laughed.

"You might have been, but Scotland wasn't. That was Elizabeth's war, and she wasn't all that popular in these parts. And before you ask, no, I don't know what 'blighted' means—although there are plenty of acres of ground on the island that have proved too difficult to work for an honest man to make a living.

"As far as I can tell, they lived there for several years. There are no records of any of them taking a wife—although that does not mean there was no fraternizing with the local women, just that none of it was sanctioned by the church.

"And there is only one other thing I can tell you. Three years after they arrived, they were all dead and buried. Their stones are out at the back end of the churchyard. They're faded and worn now, and scarcely legible, but if I have read them right, the men all died on the same date, and all have the same words inscribed beneath their names.

"'Gone to meet their maker, marching to a different drum.'"

———————————

When I switched on the radio the next morning, I heard "Spanish Harlem," quickly followed by "Spanish Eyes" and "Boots of Spanish Leather."

It seemed the period of dormancy had been broken.

4

The conversation with the minister marked the start of a new phase in my relationship with the house, as if it had peeled back another layer of the onion and taken me one step closer to the center of the mystery.

My twitch grew more pronounced. I found myself drumming out the repeater rhythm on my desk, on the kitchen table, even going so far as typing to the beat when composing emails on my laptop.

No limbs, no limbs, no head, no head, left arm gone, left leg gone, no legs, no head.

The emails were to my friends down south, thanking them for the Christmas invitations, but turning them down with a vague promise to meet up in the coming year. It was a promise I had little intention of keeping, for the house had its hold on me—the house, and Beth.

Our conversations were getting longer, at least on my side of them. I'd stand at the easel, ostensibly busy painting, with nary a brushstroke made in an hour as I called back to mind a trip to her favorite pizza place, or a night spent by the riverside watching the lights of the city twinkle on the Thames. She didn't reply, but I was coming to think I could hear a whisper, just at the edge of hearing, soft and sibilant, like her breathing in my ear.

I began to hear the beat everywhere—in the tapping of the sparrows on the windows, in the drumming of rain against the roof, in the lap of waves on the shore. At nights before sleeping, I'd listen to my heart pound in my ears and imagine it matching the rhythm my fingers drummed out on the sheets.

When Christmas Eve came round, I rang up Alan, intending to plead illness and cancel. I felt like I would be abandoning Beth. But he would hear none of it.

"Listen, I'm not taking the flak from my mother—she'll have been slaving away in the kitchen all day today. And if you don't turn up, she'll just make me eat even more. It could get messy. There could be an explosion. We'll see you at one. Don't be late. Okay?"

Even then I almost didn't leave the next morning—partly because of the house, and partly through embarrassment that I had totally failed to buy a present. In a moment of madness, I took the abstract painting off the easel, wrapped it up in some brown paper I had kept from the move, and took it with me across the island.

The wheel noise on the wet road surface kept time with my fingers drumming on the steering wheel.

No limbs, no limbs, no head, no head, left arm gone, left leg gone, no legs, no head.

The family thanked me for the painting. Alan's mum was most effusive about the gift, at least until it was unwrapped. Several things showed in their expressions when they saw the work—confusion mainly, and also just a hint of disgust. They were too polite to mention it but I had a feeling the fruits of my autumn spent painting was destined for the back of a cupboard never to be spoken of again.

Fortunately that was the only sour note in what turned out to be a Christmas as good as any I remembered from my childhood. Alan's mum did us all proud with a feast fit for the chiefs of Dunvegan, while his dad kept our glasses topped up with fine local ales and some heady Australian wine. I was quite relaxed by the time we left the table, and even put up with a game of charades where I did not know half of the shows or personalities Alan's parents played out.

Alan surprised me by taking to the piano and belting out some standards before leading us in carols that even I knew the words to sing along to. Then we did indeed have a snooze while a Bond movie played on the television, before heading out into a cold night for the shindig at the George Hotel.

The promised dance turned out to be more of a full-scale party to which it seemed everyone in town had been invited. Local lasses whirled Alan and me around the floor, songs were sung, games were played and everybody had a high old time.

Somewhere around midnight, I went outside for some air. I spotted the old woman and her son immediately. They stood in the corner of the car park, as if they had been there all along, waiting for me.

I walked, rather more unsteadily than I would have wished, toward them.

"You're drunk," the man said.

"Yes, and you're ugly, but I'll be sober in the morning."

The ancient joke went completely over his head. The old woman didn't seem too amused either. She stared into my eyes, then took my left hand in both of hers. My fingers twitched, seemingly eager to beat the rhythm. She dropped my hand as if she'd been burned.

"You've left it too late," she said, her eyes sad. "Much too late."

The man led her away.

"Hey, wait," I shouted, but they seemed to scuttle off, like fleeing sparrows, leaving me alone in the corner of the square.

As I walked back toward the hotel entrance, it started to snow.

––––––––––––

I woke the next morning—or more accurately, afternoon—to Alan banging about in his kitchen singing "White Christmas" at the top of his voice. I was vaguely aware that the party had gone on long into the night, and I remembered our footprints in fresh snow on the short walk from the hotel to Alan's flat, but beyond that, most of the time after midnight was little more than a blur.

I remembered the old woman's words well enough though.

"You've left it too late."

"Breakfast?" Alan shouted.

"Just some toast and coffee—lots of coffee," I replied, and groaned as I tried to get out of the sofa that had taken a death grip on my back and neck.

"I could make a full fry-up?" he said, but the thought of all that oily food made my stomach roil. I stumbled to the bathroom, had a shower and felt almost human again.

Three cups of coffee and some toast got the engine running, but it almost stalled when Alan suggested a hair of the dog.

"The George will be open," he said. "Fancy a pint or three?"

Actually, I did, but I also knew that if I started, I wouldn't get home that day, and the house had been calling me since I woke up.

"Maybe at the New Year," I said. "I've got to get back."

Alan pointed out the window. I noticed, for the first time, that it was still snowing—not heavy, but persistent.

"You might not make it. The council won't be out today—it's a holiday for them, too—and the roads won't have been gritted. It might be best to stay here a wee bit longer?"

"Stay and get pissed again? I'm not sure my liver would stand it."

"Mum's got a fridge full of leftovers too—we could take on plenty of ballast?"

I laughed.

"Don't tempt me, but I need to get back. There's some folks down south I need to talk to online, and I said I'd phone Beth's parents."

That little lie made me uncomfortable. Beth's parents and I hadn't spoken since the funeral, and we both liked the situation just fine, but Alan didn't know that. He relented, and let me off with the promise that we'd meet up at some point for the New Year festivities.

I went out into a snow-covered landscape.

Portree was eerily quiet, considering it was already two o' clock in the afternoon. An old man walked a wheezing dog, and said something to me as he passed, but his accent was so broad I didn't catch it, and I just muttered something in reply, hoping I hadn't been rude.

As I got to the car park, I checked the far corner, half expecting the woman and her son to be standing there, watching me, but there was only a stretch of unbroken snow leading up the incline away from the town center.

I had to brush snow from the windshield, and my hands felt like blocks of ice by the time I finally got in and started the car up. At least it started on cue, although the wheels spun rather alarmingly as I pulled out, and I almost didn't make it up the incline that led to the Edinbane and Dunvegan road, sliding left and right and struggling for traction all the way.

I was on the verge of turning back and throwing myself on Alan's ample hospitality when I crested the hill and the snow thinned enough for the wheels to get a better grip. I was still doing little more than fifteen miles an hour, but at least I was making progress, so I pressed on.

I quickly regretted that decision. The snow fell harder, testing the limits of my wipers, and I crawled forward, peering into a white emptiness. There was no other traffic on the road—the locals weren't that stupid—and I was starting to have thoughts of being stranded out here for the day, to be found, dead and frozen, once everyone else had stopped partying.

As if in reply to my pessimism, my left hand drummed out the repeating beat on the steering wheel. The engine took up the beat, wheels alternately, gripping then sliding on the road surface in an almost balletic bump and grind. By the time we went through Edinbane, the wipers had joined in, and I was singing at the top of my voice, a nonsense scat vocal, but one that perfectly stayed in time. The snow came in waves, on beat, against the windshield and we danced all the way home.

I was quite exhausted by the time I pulled into the barn. It was getting dim—the forty-five minutes it normally took me had stretched and elongated into almost two hours in the snow, but I had a smile on my face as I got out of the car and turned toward the house.

There was somebody waiting for me, out on the shore, obscured in the midst of a whirling funnel of snow and spray, standing right where the old crofter's cottage used to be.

Beth?

I ran across the snow-covered yard, noticing, despite my haste, that mine were the only footprints.

Beth?

I could almost touch her. She had her back to me, and wore a long cloak that reached from neck to ankles. Her hair was up, in a tight bun pinned by a single piece of what looked like white bone, and she seemed shorter somehow, more stocky.

But who else could it be?

I reached forward, arms wide, eager for an embrace.

A wind got up off the loch, whipping spray and sleet into my face. I brushed it away with my sleeve and blinked.

I was alone on the shore, standing on the fresh rubble above the filled-in root cellar.

I spent the next hour standing at the French windows, looking out over the shore. All I saw was snow and spray, but I stood there until the light went out of the sky completely. The snow turned to sleet that washed down the windows, turning everything into a soft-focus blur. I finally turned away when rain started beating the repeating pattern on the window.

That night, I heard the pattern everywhere—in the rushing water when I ran the tap, in the hum of the microwave as I heated a pizza, in the crackle and hiss as damp logs burned in the fireplace, and in the constant drumming of sleety rain against the windows. My fingers beat against the arm of the sofa in sympathetic rhythm.

No limbs, no limbs, no head, no head, left arm gone, left leg gone, no legs, no head.

When I realized that I was now also tapping my foot in time, I made a conscious effort to take control. I fetched a beer from the fridge and set off a movie on the laptop—a big, overblown and bombastic Hollywood mind-number.

The explosions kept time with the beat.

When the movie finished, the laptop, without any intervention on my part, started up my program, but only playing the eight repeater parts. I switched off the machine and pulled the power cord from the socket.

I went to bed with the beat thudding in my chest and ears.

I couldn't sleep. The storm ramped up outside. Snow spattered against the bedroom window and a gale howled, strong enough to cause the hatchway in the ceiling above my bed to rattle.

No limbs, no limbs, no head, no head, left arm gone, left leg gone, no legs, no head.

Tormentor

I drifted in a half-awake, half-asleep doze, scarcely aware that my fingers were drumming on the bedclothes, my legs twitching. I was lost in a dance, and this time I was not going to be able to escape for air.

No limbs, no limbs, no head, no head, left arm gone, left leg gone, no legs, no head.

Shadows capered and swirled on the ceiling, impossible shadows, for there was no moonlight to cast them, just snow and wind and the waters of the loch that now splashed in step on the rocks of the shore. A light went on in the main living area, dim, flickering and diffuse. The laptop program started up, beeping the beats in an impossibly loud chorus far beyond the range of the machine's speakers. The whole house shook and rattled.

No limbs, no limbs, no head, no head, left arm gone, left leg gone, no legs, no head.

The bed bounced in time. Above the cacophony, I heard the quietest of creaks in the doorway and turned my head.

She stood there, silhouetted against the flickering from the laptop, a dim, almost smoky figure, her cape draped around her.

I stretched out my arms.

She came to me.

5

The next morning dawned crisp and clear. I woke when the sparrows started tapping on the bedroom window. I felt groggy, decidedly hungover, and confused. I could still feel her against my body, the weight and heft of reality; I smelled her hair, tasted the salt on the skin at her neck. It hadn't been Beth—it was sex, pure, simple, fantasy sex, and I felt as if I'd just betrayed Beth's memory.

It was only a dream.

I staggered into the living area. The laptop was switched off, the cord still unplugged from the wall—never mind that I knew for a fact I'd already erased the beeping program. Outside the French windows the snow lay, several inches thick now, the only tracks in it the small scribbling left by the sparrows' dances. I half expected to see her standing there over the rubble of the cottage cellar, but there was just the flat, cold, calm loch, a fine mist wafting across it like a thin veil.

Over the morning, I started to build a rationalized story in my head—one that involved too little sleep, too much booze and just the right confluence of old stories and coincidences to come to a head with an appearance of the woman in my bed. By lunchtime I had convinced myself it was no more than a fugue state, a momentary lapse in my critical faculties.

I made a sandwich and a pot of coffee, dressed warmly, and went out onto the patio to try to clear my head. I looked over to the woodpile, hoping for a sight of my little friendly stoat.

He wouldn't ever be joining me in the mornings again. The small body lay draped over the topmost log, covered by a thin layer of snow. I went over for a closer look. The poor thing was frozen stiff to the wood, small eyes staring at me, accusingly.

———————

I spent the rest of the day catching up with friends online. They'd had a variety of festive periods—family fights, stuck in airports, big party that was still ongoing, two new best friends and one impending divorce. Just like any other Christmas. I told them about the dance in Portree, and Alan's mum's cooking, and they made the appropriate displays of jealousy, but no one asked about Beth, and I didn't—I couldn't—speak of my nocturnal visitor.

"It was just a dream," I told the urn on the mantel. "It didn't mean anything."

I found that I was hungry, ravenously so. The meager fare in my fridge and cupboards couldn't compare to what was on offer at Alan's parents', but I managed to get a meat stew going, the aromas filling the house most of the afternoon and early evening. I built a fire in the grate after fetching fresh wood. I had to move the log to which the stoat was frozen to one side, unsure how to dispose of the tiny body, leaving the decision for another time. By the time I served up the stew, it was getting dark again outside. I closed the curtains against the night and tried to lose myself in a book.

It wasn't long before I noticed my left-hand fingers drumming on the book's spine.

I put on the radio, listening to old favorites telling even older jokes on Radio 4, but whereas I usually found them amusing, tonight they sounded mocking—aging chimps chattering to other aging chimps about the follies of the young. I switched to a classical station and got something Russian, but the rhythm all too quickly synchronized with my finger-drummer. I tried a movie—rugged individual wisecracks his way through a tired old plot to save the U.S. president and get his wife back.

I wish it were that easy.

The urn on the mantel rattled in time to the gunfire, my fingers drummed the repeater beat, and the pressure in my head grew and grew until it was all I could do not to scream.

I drew back the curtains and stared out over the moonlit loch. It all looked so calm and serene, an opposite to the storm of the night before. Silver glistened on the ice-crisp snow, myriad dancing sparkles mirroring the starry sky above. I went outside to revel in the dark beauty of it, ignoring the chill that immediately threatened to knife all the way down to bone, willing to endure it for some seconds of magic.

My fingers finally stilled and my head emptied of everything but the sea and stars. I stood there as long as I could, allowing silence to fill me, before the cold finally drove me inside. Not even the accusing eyes of the stoat could dent my feeling of peace in that perfect moment.

It didn't last, of course. Nothing does. But that night I had the best night's sleep for several months, and I woke refreshed.

I found a soot mark on the bathroom mirror the next morning.

No head, right leg missing.

The days between the resuming of the soot marks and the New Year passed in a blur. The marks appeared with increasing regularity, not confined to first thing in the morning, and turning up all over the house. It took most of my energy, and then some more, to keep pace. I started drinking more heavily, trying to blot out the ever-increasing drumming that was building again, and threatening to turn me into a quivering, twitching mess. Standing outside the patio door always calmed me, for a time at least, but it never took long for my hand to twitch and drum and the repeater to start up again.

No limbs, no limbs, no head, no head, left arm gone, left leg gone, no legs, no head.

You may ask why I stayed. In those days just after Christmas I regularly asked myself the same question. At first it was because I found I was tired of running, and that a part of me wondered whether everything that was happening was unfinished business between Beth and me.

Later, I stayed because I didn't have any choice in the matter.

As I said, I started drinking a lot—half a bottle of Talisker and a handful of beers most days, enough to ensure my sleep would be more akin to a coma and therefore undisturbed by visitors.

I woke on the morning of the thirtieth of December to find the whole bathroom wall covered in soot marks. It had got so that I could immediately pick out the repeater among the chaos. It was there, three times.

More messages I did not know what to do with.

I logged on to the laptop, thinking of starting to catalogue this new phenomenon, maybe even start a new grid. I didn't have to. It was there in a new email—a hundred and twenty-eight lines of eight figures, the repeater clearly standing out thirteen times. I gave in to the inevitable and rewrote my program, coding it to play this latest message. I changed the beeps to a drumbeat sound I downloaded from an online source—a kettledrum, big, meaty and deep in the bass register. I hooked the laptop up to my stereo system speakers and started the program. I left the volume low, but even then I heard it anywhere I went in the house, whispering straight into my bones.

No limbs, no limbs, no head, no head, left arm gone, left leg gone, no legs, no head.

I took the whisky bottle outside, closed the doors behind me and stood, back to the windows, staring sightlessly out across the loch as the glass vibrated in rhythm against my spine.

6

The morning of the last day of the old year brought thick mist across the loch. I'd had no real sleep to speak of for several days and existed in a mental fog that perfectly matched the weather. The laptop kept up an incessant accompaniment to my whisky-induced headache, and the urn on the mantel danced in sympathy.

At least the soot marks had stopped again, now that the long message had been delivered, but there had, as yet, been no answer to the incessant drumbeats from the stereo system, and I was unsure how much longer my frayed nerves were going to last.

I took coffee and toast out onto the patio and sat there, getting damp in the fog being preferable to being indoors with the drumming. A pair of sparrows came down and waited for me to drop some crumbs, but even they seemed somehow dull and puppet-like, almost parodies of their former excitable selves. The stoat still glared at me with a frozen, dead stare, as if I had been at fault for the vagaries of the weather that had brought its doom, and the waters of the loch lapped listlessly against the rocks.

No limbs, no limbs, no head, no head, left arm gone, left leg gone, no legs, no head.

My phone rang while I was drinking my coffee but I didn't answer. The caller ID said it was Alan, and he'd just want to know what I was planning for the festivities. I had no plans, beyond going slowly crazy and drinking what little booze I had left in the house, but if I told him that, he'd only try to get me to go to a party, and I was in no fit state to face polite, or even impolite, company.

81

I finished the coffee and, rather than go back inside, took a stroll down to the shore. I was thinking of the summer, and the glorious day out on the water fishing. It seemed like a lifetime ago, and felt like a story someone had told me rather than something I had experienced. I knew the details, but I couldn't conjure up any of the emotions; the magic had gone, been sucked out of me by the rhythm. I came to a halt at the realization, wondering how I had got so jaded, so quickly.

The drumbeat got louder. The volume control on the stereo had just been twisted, and the house pounded out the rhythm at my back, faster now, more insistent, an imperative I could not ignore.

I felt it, throbbing even through the soles of my feet. I looked down.

I stood on the rubble, right on top of the old root cellar of the crofter's cottage. The beat got louder still, pounding like a fist against my skull, jarring every bone in my body as it came up from below.

There was one last repeated eight, then it cut off, as if someone indoors had pulled the plug.

I looked down at my feet again. The rubble had been loosened, and I had sunk a good six inches into a new hollow over the top of the cellar.

I had just received another message.

I wasted no time in getting started, and at first it was simple enough. By kneeling at the side of the cellar I could bend, lift a stone or handful of pebbles, and toss them over my shoulder onto the shore, some of them even getting as far as the water where my digging was accompanied by infrequent splashes. But after only ten minutes of that my shoulders ached, my fingers were numb and frozen, and dampness soaked my trousers from ankle to thigh. And I had barely made a dent in the rubble that choked the cellar. I was going to be of no use at all if I developed hypothermia.

Reluctantly, I stood and made for the house, casting glances over my shoulder, expecting to see her standing there, waiting for my return.

I dressed more appropriately—my painting overalls over the top of dry trousers and shirt, gloves and hat, and extra-thick socks under my walking boots. Even as I did so, I was aware it was stupid to even contemplate what I intended in the middle of an island winter, but the last message had been forceful, and my fingers already itched to be drumming. As I said before, I had little conscious choice in the matter.

When I went back out, I took a skillet and a heavy-duty pan with me. I didn't have a spade, and I couldn't think of anything else I could use to any great effect. The skillet did indeed work very well at first. I made good progress in excavating a hole almost a foot deep, but by this time it was already obvious it was going to be a long, dirty job; rubble and gravel clogged the cellar, and was frozen solid in places, running wet damp in others. It was heavy work, and my arms ached far too quickly. I was driven inside in the early afternoon in search of food, dry clothes, heat and a period of rest.

I ate a perfunctory sandwich, changed my shirt and trousers, and got a fire going in the grate. When I sat down on the sofa, the stereo system kicked in with the drumbeats—not too loud, but enough to let me know the job wasn't nearly done. The urn rattled on the mantel, and I imagined Beth's voice.

Are you just going to sit there?

As I stood, my phone rang—Alan again. I ignored it and went back to my digging.

––––––––––––

The next hours passed in a blur of digging and shoveling rubble out of the hole. Darkness fell, early dusk exacerbated by the fog. It didn't slow me much. I drove the car out of the barn to the corner of the house and dug under the unblinking gaze of the headlights.

It got harder the deeper I got—the gravel heavy and damp, the rocks icy and slippery, the skillet cold as ice against my palms even through the gloves. I got into a rhythm of dig and remove; *no limbs, no limbs, no head, no head, left arm gone, left leg gone, no legs, no head.* It seemed to make the task go more easily, so much so that I was surprised to stop some time later and see I had more than half the hole dug out.

I had to climb my way out, struggling for grip on the edge before rolling over in the snow and standing, panting, on the shore next to a cairn of rubble. Even though the hole was only half-excavated, I saw that the black stick figures had survived their burial and still danced and capered in the car headlights on the only wall that received some light.

I staggered to the vehicle, switched off the lights to preserve the battery, and limped to the house. A shower, a change of clothes and a stiff Talisker did much to revive me, but my body felt like I had been run over by a truck. Every muscle ached and screamed in agony with each movement.

I flopped on the sofa, not intending to move unless absolutely necessary.

Fuck it. I'll do the rest tomorrow.

Somebody—or something—had other ideas. The stereo started up the beat, softly at first, a gentle reminder that this was no time for slacking. I rolled off the couch and pulled the plug on both the stereo and the laptop.

The room trembled. Like a giant heart beating, the floor vibrated underfoot. I counted it out in my head, an automatic reflex now.

No limbs, no limbs, no head, no head, left arm gone, left leg gone, no legs, no head.

Beth's urn danced and rattled on the mantel as the beat got stronger, inching perilously close to the edge. I wasn't going to be able to reach it in time to stop it falling onto the hard stone of the hearth.

"Enough. I get the message," I shouted. "I'm going."

I dragged my weary limbs back outside.

Afterward I had little recollection of it. I dug. The hole got bigger; I grew more tired. At some point the car headlights dimmed and died. I fetched the flashlight and kept digging. When the battery went, I dug in what little light there was coming through the French windows from the dining room.

I dug, until there was no more left to dig. My eyes had adjusted enough that I could see the black markings on the walls of the cellar, but in the darkness I could not make out any detail, and I was too tired to think, almost too tired to stand. If my legs had given way at that point, I might have been found, days later, frozen in the cellar, as stiff and cold and accusing as the stoat on the woodpile.

It took me three attempts to pull myself up out of the hole, using up the very last vestiges of my endurance. I crawled in the snow to the patio doors, rolled inside, dragged my body over onto the sofa and was asleep, dead to the world, seconds later.

7

I woke to pounding—a heavy thumping that in my confused state sounded like another summons to the digging.

"Fuck off, I'm done," I shouted.

"Jim? Are you okay?"

It was Alan. He sounded far away. The pounding started again.

"Come on, Jim. Let me in. It's bloody freezing out here."

I finally came fully awake. He was at the front door.

"Hold on, I'm coming."

I got up off the sofa too fast and had to hold on to the mantel to avoid falling to the floor. Using the wall and furniture I was able to stay upright until I got to the door and opened it wide, just in time to see a taxi depart back down the track.

"Happy New Year," Alan said, and thrust a bottle of whisky at me. His smile turned to shock as he looked me up and down.

"For God's sake, Jim. What's happened here?"

I tried to smile and nearly managed it.

"I had a wee bit of car trouble," I said.

"What did it do, try to eat you?"

I looked down at my clothes—I was caked in dirt from neck to toe, my trousers torn, shirt frayed. My hands were gray with clotted gravel, looking like a bad effect from a cheap horror movie, and I guessed my face must look the same.

I laughed, and Alan smiled back, but I could see he was concerned.

"I lost the place a bit," I said. "Bloody thing refused to start so I decided to see if a good kicking would sort it out."

"And did it work?"

"No. But I felt a damned sight better afterwards. Come on in, I'll be with you in a minute."

I left him in the kitchen while I went for a shower. Upon my return, I found him heating a takeaway in the microwave.

"Curry and Talisker," he said as I joined him. "It'll cure most anything except for a moody car." He passed me a large glass of whisky. "And in case you missed it the first time—Happy New Year."

I looked at the clock—it was two in the morning.

"I'm not dark, not handsome, but I'm tall, and I have more booze in the bag, so I'm the perfect first foot."

"I must have fallen asleep," I said.

I saw him look at the sofa, and the trail of dirt that led from there across to the patio doors.

"Cleaner's day off?" he said, and raised an eyebrow.

I knocked back the whisky in one gulp, feeling the heat warm me from the inside.

"Get me pissed enough and you might get a story before I fall asleep again," I replied.

"Best offer I've had all year," Alan said, and poured another.

On that first morning of the year, the whisky kept me fueled and I did indeed tell Alan a story—some of it was even true. I talked about Beth, how we met, how we lived and how she passed. I talked about grief, and why I kept her ashes in the urn on the mantel. I talked about why the painting I'd given his parents for Christmas was so bloody bleak and empty, and I talked about loneliness, and closure. What I didn't talk about was the house. If Alan noticed, he didn't say, and after a while we'd both had too much whisky to be attempting any rational thinking. With my confessional done, Alan took over the talking duties, keeping me amused with more tales from Portree and the lives of both the locals and the tourists who descended on the place in the summer.

At some point around sunrise, everything caught up with me and I drifted off to sleep in the middle of a tale about a policeman, a nude sunbather and a Great Dane that would have been uproariously funny if I'd been sober enough to appreciate it.

When I woke, it was dark again, and Alan was gone.

He'd left a note on the table.

Family duties call. See you next Saturday in Dunvegan?

The way I felt right then, booze was the last thing on my mind. I spent ten minutes clearing up the worst of the dirt between the sofa and the patio, put on a load of washing, and pulled up an old movie on the laptop. All the time I was aware of the reopened hole out on the shore, worrying at it like a tongue at a fresh cavity. I'd opened a door. I didn't need to have my thumbs pricked to know that something was coming through.

It was just a matter of when—and what.

PART 3: CLOSURE

1

I didn't sleep well that first night. I lay awake watching shadows crawl, alternately eyeing the ceiling and the doorway, wondering if she would be back, part of me hoping. I dozed fitfully, seeing the time on the alarm clock tick over the hours as the night drew on. I got up at four and did a circuit of the house, checking for fresh soot marks—there were none. At some point around five, I managed to get a couple of hours' sleep, but I did not feel at all rested when daylight drove the shadows away.

After a shower, I took a mug of coffee out onto the patio. The snow had melted, leaving damp grass with slushy puddles in places, mostly where I'd walked to and from the root cellar during my digging. At some point the stoat's body had disappeared from the woodpile but I had no urge to walk over to check, nor to check on the fruits of my labors in the root cellar. Just then I was content to sit on the patio and watch the play of clouds in the sky and light on the water, trying to regain some calm and stability.

It had taken me long enough, but I was beginning to understand the moods of the place, get the feel of the rhythm of the house. I was also beginning to think that my analogy of peeling away layers of an onion was closer to the truth than I had guessed. Every new manifestation seemed to take me deeper into the place's history. I have no idea where they came from, or even what they were, but somehow the house's story was being revealed, and by digging out the root cellar, I had, in effect, issued an open invitation for the story to continue. I couldn't go on considering everything to be merely booze-fed imagination. That was just too many coincidences to have to pile up in any one place. I had to accept it, and be open to whatever it was that was trying to communicate.

At least that's what I told myself. Another part of me saw it in a different light—memory and need and grief fused in a fantasy that Beth was just on the other side of a veil that I could part anytime I wanted to. I pushed that away; it felt like an even faster road to madness than the one I was on.

The only things that tried to communicate with me that morning were the sparrows. I fed them; they chirruped happily, and for a time I achieved the calm I had been searching for. I was feeling good, and the day, if a tad chilly, was a dry one. I decided to take a walk down into Dunvegan to stretch my legs and clear my head.

––––––––––

The walk took longer than usual, mostly due to having to dodge the deep, slush-filled puddles that were dotted at irregular intervals along the rutted track. A flag fluttered on the high pole above the old castle, but there was no sign of life and I didn't see any people until I was all the way down at the main crossroads in town. I bought some groceries—no more booze though—and was about to head back home when I heard a knock on glass to my right. I turned to see Alex Wark sitting in the bay window at the front of the Dunvegan. He pointed at the table in front of him—a Bible and a cup of coffee sat there. I was hoping he meant the coffee as I went in to join him.

He closed the Bible as I sat down, and ordered two more coffees.

I pointed at the book.

"How you can still believe in God when there are so many things going wrong in the world and it is obvious that he doesn't care?"

He looked up and smiled.

"The Bible says that God is love. And part of His loving nature is that He allows people to have free will. As a result, we have evil, pain and suffering, due to the choices we and others make."

"We're defined by what we do, not what He does? So I was right. He doesn't care?"

"Of course He cares. He sent His only son to die for us. That's how much He cares. He could intervene and control everything about our lives but then we would be just robots and not truly free."

"That's the bit I never got. He gives us free will. Then, when we use it, He punishes us for not doing what He wanted in the first place. That's not free will. That's tyranny."

Alex seemed to warm to the task. He smiled again as the coffees arrived, and took a long sip before continuing.

"God doesn't violate our wills by choosing us and redeeming us. Rather, He changes our hearts so that our wills choose Him."

"So, if, to be saved, I have to give up my free will, then am I even free at all? Is it really our choice to be saved if in the end we do not have the ability to choose salvation for ourselves?"

"When you accept Christ as offered in the Gospel, you receive salvation by your own decision. As such, salvation is your work. You must initiate the act. But it is also God's work, for it is God who offers salvation to you. Without Christ, there is no salvation."

"So all I have to do is ask, and it shall be given?"

"If your heart is pure. Yes."

"And there's the rub, Alex. I've got my fair share of impure thoughts, like any man. And that's something else I never understood. Why give us sensual bodies, and a full range of pleasurable activities, then tell us not to enjoy ourselves?"

"He never says not to enjoy yourself. In fact, God loves joy…when it is done with no thought of self-gratification."

"But why? Why shouldn't we gratify ourselves? Aren't we made in his image? Aren't we in fact honoring him when we do something for ourselves?"

Alex laughed.

"You've done this before, haven't you? You remind me of a Jesuit friend at the university. But if you want to joust...I think Romans says it best."

He flicked through the Bible, found the right place, and read.

"For they that are after the flesh do mind the things of the flesh; but they that are after the spirit do mind the things of the spirit. For to be carnally minded is death; but to be spiritually minded is life and peace. Because the carnal mind is enmity against God: for it is not subject to the law of God, neither indeed can be. So then they that are in the flesh cannot please God."

"Very nice. But it's just more directives from on high. It still doesn't answer why."

"There are some things you have to take on faith. I'm heading for a prayer meeting this afternoon. Perhaps you would like to join me?"

I drained my coffee.

"Thanks, but no thanks, Alex. What was it you said? 'They that are in the flesh cannot please God.' There's the thing—I'm not even interested in trying to please him. He lost that right back in a hospital room in London. I believe I'll stay on the side of the flesh for a while longer. You know where you are with that."

Alex had lost his smile now.

"You be careful, lad," he said. "You've got a quick mind, and you're imaginative. That's not always a good combination around here."

I was still mulling over the conversation as I walked along the shore. I wasn't a believer in either God or a benign universe. I grew up Church of England and went to Sunday school. None of it took.

I've prayed once in my adult life—at Beth's bedside. I prayed, not for me, but for her. She was in the final stages of dying, would be gone by morning.

I was on my knees for two hours. I prayed and I cried in equal measure. There was no catharsis. When she finally passed, I felt just as shitty as before and more than slightly disgusted with myself. Alex was the first man of God I'd talked to since a perfunctory handshake with the vicar at Beth's funeral. He hadn't convinced me to change my mind any, but I spent a while mulling over one sentence in particular.

"For they that are after the flesh do mind the things of the flesh; but they that are after the spirit the things of the spirit."

A thing of the Spirit was waiting for me when I got home. I don't think it was thinking much about God either.

2

A fog rolled in as I got close to the house, ice cold against my face, driven in waves by a breeze off the loch. I was more than happy to get inside and shut it out.

My laptop sat on the desk, open and switched on. I had an anonymous email—not garbled English this time, nor a grid of drumbeats, but a verse, in Gaelic.

Dheannain sùgradh ris a nighean duibh
N' deidh dhomh eirigh as a 'mhadainn
Dheannain sùgradh ris a nighean duibh
Dheannain sùgradh ris a'ghruagaich
'Nuair a bhiodh a' sluagh nan codal

It didn't take me long to find where it came from. It was a chorus from a folk song, its origins lost in time.

I played with the young dark-haired girl
When I woke in the morning
I played with the young dark-haired girl
I played with the long-haired girl
When everyone was asleep

As I read, the verse's rhythms synchronized in my head with the drumming of my fingers on the desk.

I found myself chanting, almost singing the short verse throughout the day as I wandered around the house. I had one of my intermittent bouts of cleaning; I vacuumed and dusted, did all the laundry, and cleared the sink of dishes and cutlery. And all the time the verse, melded now in my mind with the repeater rhythm, went round and round in my head.

In late afternoon I rewarded myself with a microwave pizza and a beer. I sat at the dining table, looking out the closed windows at the foggy scene beyond. I'd changed the view again with my placement of the cairn of rubble I had excavated from the root cellar. It sat on the edge of the shore, a squat pyramid, dark against the fog behind it. It drew my gaze so often while I was finishing the pizza that in the end I rose and closed the view off by drawing the curtains. What I couldn't close off was the Gaelic verse, a new earworm going round and round in my head, worse than any pop song or advertising ditty, a constant whisper that seemed to be a warning of the night still to come.

'Nuair a bhiodh a' sluagh nan codal; when everyone was asleep.

I put off going to bed for as long as I could. I watched two more movies and drank, coffee rather than beer or Scotch. All that meant was that I knew there would be a wakeup call from my bladder in the early hours of the morning, which only added to my trepidation.

I opened the patio doors and looked outside around midnight. There was nothing to see but fog—even the new cairn was lost in the soft gray darkness. I wasn't in the least tempted to venture outside. I closed the windows and the curtains, had a shower and went to bed.

Sleep was the last thing on my mind, but I was physically exhausted after my trials on Hogmanay, then the subsequent drinking, walking and cleaning. I had hoped that would be enough to send me to the land of Nod, but it wasn't to be.

The shadows danced and swayed on the ceiling, keeping time to the chant that continued to echo in the void in my brain. It was all I could think about.

Dheannain sùgradh ris a'ghruagaich
'Nuair a bhiodh a' sluagh nan codal

I waited for my dark-haired girl to come.

My fingers drummed the rhythm on the sheets. My legs twitched in time. I danced, lying there on the bed, keeping the beat with my partner in the shadows. Shimmering luminescence flitted across the window, as if something moved just out of sight on the shore. I couldn't get out of bed to look; the chant had me struck immobile.

The shimmering poured into the room like an incoming tide, blue and gray and silver, all dancing. The stereo started up in the main room.

No limbs, no limbs, no head, no head, left arm gone, left leg gone, no legs, no head.

The Gaelic chant swelled, roaring in my ears in accompaniment. A deeper shadow moved in the doorway; she stood there, the lady in the cloak, her hair no longer pinned up but streaming in a swathe across her shoulders, black as pitch.

I opened my arms. She came to me.

Dheannain sùgradh ris a'ghruagaich

'Nuair a bhiodh a' sluagh nan codal.

I played with my long-haired girl when everyone was asleep.

Again I felt her body against mine, cold as the fog yet heavy, most definitely alive. She lifted her head to look at me, her hair falling away from her face — green eyes, deep as rock pools, lips the palest of pale, almost blue.

We kissed. As our lips met, she fell into me, cold and mist and blue mixing like oil paints on a board, ice in my veins.

I fell into a darkness where there was only the beat, only the dance.

I was lost, forever dancing.

In the morning I could scarcely look at the mantel and at Beth's urn, sitting there, accusing me. She'd been dead these years past, but it didn't make me feel any less sure that I'd just betrayed her. Again.

"I'm sorry," I whispered.

My laptop pinged. I had mail. It was just one word.

Deeper.

I headed for the car, intending to drive into Portree to the hardware store for a pick or a shovel, but I'd forgotten about running the battery down. The engine coughed and spluttered twice. It almost took, then quit permanently. I took out my phone to call for a taxi. It started to beep at me, taking up the now-familiar rhythm.

No limbs, no limbs, no head, no head, left arm gone, left leg gone, no legs, no head.

Even from inside the car I heard the stereo start up, filling the house with the drumbeat, sending my gut vibrating in sympathy.

I got the message.

The beat got louder still as I put on the overalls, gloves and hat, but lessened to a whisper, no less insistent, when I lifted the skillet and headed out to the shore. I went down to the root cellar, climbed in, and started to dig into the hard-packed earth.

3

It took several minutes to crack the top surface, and I thought I was in for a long, hard day's work, but the hard-packed earth proved little more than a crust above much softer, wetter ground. I dug quickly through layers of soil interlaced with blacker patches that were obvious signs of fires—many fires, over many years. Twice the skillet clinked on fragments of clay pots, and a third time on a piece of rusted iron that might have been a short sword many centuries past.

Still I dug—two feet and more down while the stick figures on the cellar walls danced in the shifting shadows. The soil got heavier, a dark peat sodden with water. I was cold, wet and filthy; my arms ached and my head pounded along with the whispering beat of the drums.

I screamed in frustration as the drumbeat got louder. I raised the skillet and brought it down, hard in the soft peat.

I hit something. The drums beat faster and my digging matched the new rhythm, throwing up damp piles of peat, sloshing icy brown water everywhere until I had it uncovered. I looked down at what looked to be a rolled tube of decaying leather lying at the bottom of a dark muddy pool.

The drums fell quiet.

I had to climb down into the new hole to fetch my discovery, cold water gripping me from ankles to balls, turning my legs to stone. I heaved the leather up out of the hole and dragged myself up after it. Even then I wasn't done. I lifted the leather tube out of the cellar, rolling it up onto the surface, but when I tried to pull myself out after it, my legs gave way beneath me and I fell back, splashing in an inch of mud and slush.

The drums started to beat insistently again.

"Okay, okay—I'm doing it," I shouted.

It took all my strength, and I did it using mainly my arms, for my legs seemed to have turned to soft putty, but after an interminable scramble, I pulled myself out of the cellar and rolled to lie alongside the thing I had brought up out of the hole.

It was only then that I had my first good look at it. It looked like a four-foot-long sausage—one that had been cooked, then left in the fridge too long. It had been burnt at one time, judging by the blackened areas and charring that was clearly visible, but whatever it contained had been rolled tight. There seemed to be at least three visible layers of leather, and possibly more waiting to be uncovered.

The drums beat a staccato rhythm, pounding the repeater beat into my skull. I knew what was being asked.

With a tired groan, I lifted the leather tube—more water ran inside my sleeves but didn't make me much wetter than I already was—and staggered, bent almost double, up to the house and in through the patio doors. I trailed a spattered pattern of mud and water into the house and dropped the thing with a wet smack on the dining room table.

The drums fell silent, the only sound coming from a steady drip from the table to the floor.

I stripped naked in the bathroom and stood under a hot shower for ten minutes until I was completely rid of the numbing cold. My arms and legs tingled and became bright red, but it was an improvement from the gray-blue I had seen there before the shower.

While I was putting on some dry clothes, I started to feel the chill again. I went back to the main room and lit a fire in the grate, piling on as many logs as I could manage until the flames roared and waves of heat drove me back. I poured a large Talisker, gulped down half of it, and took the rest over to have a closer look at what I'd brought in.

It was already drying out. The top layer was cracked and almost brittle. I peeled back a piece of it and it came away in my hand, crumpling under my skin to a mushy pulp. I was afraid to do any more exploring in case the whole thing fell apart on me, so I left it dripping on the table and returned to the sofa to rest my weary limbs.

What had I just done? The message had been clear enough—*Dig until I tell you to stop.* Well, I'd done it, and found something. Had I reached the center, the truth at the heart of the mystery? At that precise moment, I was too tired and too confused to care.

I was asleep within seconds.

When I woke, it was dark again. I was sweating, sitting in a red room; flickering flames from the dying fire cast scarlet and black shadows to all corners. Drums—several of them—beat in the far distance where a soft voice sang in accompaniment.

'Nuair a bhiodh a' sluagh nan codal; when everyone was asleep.

But whatever was in the room with me was no Celtic lady. I felt its anger, a red rage to match any flame. I tried to get off the couch, but my torso was squeezed and constricted. It sat on my chest, breathing its hate in my face, and I could only lie there and take it as the drums beat and the flames flickered.

Sweat ran into my right eye, stinging, blurring the room into a wash of color. The drumming intensified, shaking the walls and rattling the windows. The stereo kicked in—"Spanish Harlem"

100

again, then, so loud as to be almost deafening, "Boots of Spanish Leather."

Dylan wailed, a drum crashed a final beat that shook the house to its foundations, and the weight on my chest lifted as the patio doors blew open.

A chill breeze wafted the fire back to life and I sat up, gasping for air.

My laptop flickered as it booted up and I heard the ping of incoming email.

4

I had another grid for my program—screeds of it this time, eight columns and over six hundred lines. Fortunately I'd set the thing up so that it was a relatively simple matter to get the grid into the program's small database. I got it running, hooked it up to the stereo, and left it to play softly in the background while I had a shower and shave and rustled up some breakfast.

I was so used to the beat by now it was almost soothing. The terror I'd felt on wakening faded to little more than the memory of a bad dream. Beth's urn rattled on the mantel, as if dancing to the beat. I took some coffee and toast onto the patio. As I walked past the dining room table I saw that the leather bundle was cracked and dry, almost toasted by the fire. I'd tackle that after breakfast.

I had a feeling the end was close now.

I had my last breakfast in the house sitting on the patio watching a misty dawn over the loch with drums beating softly as a backdrop. My sparrow friends came down and danced at my feet as I fed them crumbs.

I had a final look at the view, drained my coffee, and went to have a closer look at what I'd brought up out of the hole.

Boots of Spanish Leather.

It was obvious that the leather, even old and cracked as it now was, had at one time been rather fine, embroidered as it was with scenes of sailboats and docks. It may have been Spanish, but I did not get that confirmed until I unrolled four layers, each of which

102

was in better condition than the last, and finally revealed what lay inside. A distant drumbeat started up, rumbling from afar, as I peeled back the last section.

At first it looked like little more than a jumble of bone and silver, until my mind processed what I was seeing.

It had been a burial, sometime in the deep past—a man of some import at that. His skull, grimacing from bottomless eye sockets, was mostly intact, as were two femurs.

Skull and crossed bones.

He'd been interred with a cloak that had once been an animal skin but was now little more than fragments of tattered hide and fur. There was also a gold bracelet, finely carved and looking too delicate to touch for fear of it falling apart, and a two-foot-long tusk, ivory by the look of it and walrus at a guess.

Lying draped on the tusk was proof of the Spaniards' presence—two silver crucifixes on long chains had been wrapped around the ivory. I could make a good guess at what had happened. The Spaniards had found the grave and given the remains a Christian burial in the rolls of leather, possibly in the hope of bringing peace to an errant spirit.

The fire flared and the drums beat louder as I bent for a better look at the tusk.

It was scrimshaw, carved with delicate strokes. I unwound the crucifixes and dropped them among the bones as I lifted it into a better light.

A ring of runic script circled the thick end, and there was a fine depiction of a warrior chief wielding an axe that showed clearly enough who the owner of the piece had been. The length of the tusk was carved in stick figures.

No limbs, no limbs, no head, no head, left arm gone, left leg gone, no legs, no head.

I looked from them, to the figure with the axe, and down to the grinning skull lying on the table. The figures weren't a message at all, nor were they a code for a drummer to follow—they were depictions of a warrior's exploits in battle.

No limbs, no limbs, no head, no head, left arm gone, left leg gone, no legs, no head.

The drums got louder and the fire flared again. A single line of soot drew down the whitewashed wall to my left, then another. The stereo kicked in, full volume, and the house shook again, rocking to the beat. In my mind's eye, I saw a bloodied axe swinging in time.

More soot figures appeared, marching across the wall in ranks. The drums pounded and the fire blazed, sending waves of heat through the room. My chest felt tight, breathing getting more difficult. I wrapped the crucifixes around the tusk and laid it back down among the bones.

The drums didn't lessen. The pounding got heavier. A crack ran the full length of the ceiling above me; plaster and dust fell like fine mist. Beth's urn danced on the mantel, threatening to topple. I moved toward it, but the heat of the flames drove me away.

More stick figures marched across the walls. The floor bucked and swayed in time to the beat, threatening to throw me off my feet. Beth's urn did a final bump and grind and toppled to smash in the grate. Her ashes rose and swirled as the heat caught them.

The Spaniards had tried to make the chief stay down by giving him a Christian burial, but I knew a better way, a way that had kept Beth at peace these past years. She had just reminded me of it.

Ashes to ashes, stardust to stardust.

I swept the roll of leather, bones, cloak and bracelet into the grate where it took immediately, flames roiling beyond the confines of the fireplace and lapping up the walls. The drums pounded; it sounded like rage. I had to back away as the sofa caught fire, blazing like a small furnace within seconds. Something fluttered down from above—the girl's notebook, dislodged from its spot in the rafters, catching fire as it fell and blackened to ash in seconds.

The book of folk tales went next, falling from the mantle into the blaze, taking the tale of the Little Drummer Boy with it.

The whole room raged in red flame. A floorboard cracked beneath me, then another. The drumbeat pounded in my head threatening to drive me into oblivion. I staggered backward, reaching the patio doors as the flames found the curtains and sent them up in a sheet of fire. I backed out into the yard just as part of the roof caved in and sent a shower of sparks high into the air.

I threw the logs of my wood supply through the patio doors, stoking the fire further as the drums beat and the red rage screamed. The stoat's frozen body lay at the foot of the pile, and I threw that in, too, it blazed briefly before joining everything else in a conflagration that ate the house in time to the pounding beat.

I thought it would never go quiet, but as the last of the roof fell in and a huge shower of sparks was thrown up to be taken away by the wind, the drums finally fell silent. I was left on the shore, with only the whistling of the wind off the loch for company.

A thin plume of smoke rose from the wreckage. Fine ash fell around me, all that was left of my home, of the chief who had slept there all these years—of Beth.

Ashes to ashes, stardust to stardust.

5

I'm writing this some six months after those events. It's summer, and here in Edinburgh the tourists have arrived with the sun. I've started painting again—abstracts mostly. It's hard going as my hand wants to draw stick figures, and every so often I find myself drumming out the beat.

No limbs, no limbs, no head, no head, left arm gone, left leg gone, no legs, no head.

I keep in touch with Alan. He wants me to sell the land; he says I could make at least some of my money back. But the cash isn't as important as my peace of mind. I cannot be sure I finished the job. Who is to say that I reached the center of the mystery? Was the chief the first to hear the drums? Or is there something deeper still on that loch shore, lurking, waiting for someone else to answer the call?

All I know is it will not be me.

I was lost in the dance, and no doubt I will be again, when I join Beth, wherever she might be.

But not yet.

About the Author

William Meikle is a Scottish writer, now living in Canada, with over thirty novels published in the genre press and more than 300 short story credits in thirteen countries. He has books available from a variety of publishers including Dark Regions Press and Severed Press and his work has appeared in a large number of professional anthologies and magazines. He lives in Newfoundland with whales, bald eagles and icebergs for company. When he's not writing he drinks beer, plays guitar, and dreams of fortune and glory.

BIBLIOGRAPHY

NOVELS

The Green and The Black / Crossroad Press
The Boathouse / Crossroad Press
Ramskull / Crossroad Press
Songs of Dreaming Gods / Crossroad Press
The Dunfield Terror / Crossroad Press
Fungoid / Crossroad Press
The Hole / Crossroad Press
The Exiled / Crossroad Press
Night of the Wendigo / Crossroad Press
The Ravine / Dark Regions Press
The Invasion / Dark Regions Press
The Valley / Dark Regions Press
The Creeping Kelp / Dark Regions Press
Crustaceans / Dark Regions Press
Sherlock Holmes: The Dreaming Man / Gryphonwood Press
Berserker / Gryphonwood Press
The Midnight Eye Files: The Amulet / Gryphonwood Press
The Midnight Eye Files: The Sirens / Gryphonwood Press

The Midnight Eye Files: The Skin Game / Gryphonwood Press
The Concordances of the Red Serpent / Gryphonwood Press
Watchers: The Coming of the King / Gryphonwood Press
Watchers: The Battle for the Throne / Gryphonwood Press
Watchers: Culloden / Gryphonwood Press
Watchers: Omnibus edition / Gryphonwood Press
Eldren: The Book of the Dark / Gryphonwood Press
Island Life / Gryphonwood Press
The Road Hole Bunker Mystery - Charade Media

NOVELLAS
Operation: North Pole / Severed Press
Operation: Orkney / Severed Press
Operation: Patagonia / Severed Press
Operation: London / Severed Press
Operation: Sahara / Severed Press
Operation: Yukon / Severed Press
Operation: North Sea / Severed Press
Operation: Congo / Severed Press
Operation: Mongolia / Severed Press
Operation: Norway / Severed Press
Operation: Syria / Severed Press
Operation: Loch Ness / Severed Press
Operation: Amazon / Severed Press
Operation: Siberia/ Severed Press
Operation: Antarctica / Severed Press
Infestation / Severed Press
The Lost Valley / Severed Press
Sea Hunters: Shonisaurus / Severed Press
The Land Below / Severed Press
The Sea Below / Severed Press
The City Below / Severed Press
Tormentor / Crossroad Press
Clockwork Dolls / Crossroad Press

Sigils and Totems: A Collection of Novellas / Crossroad Press
Broken Sigil / Crossroad Press
Pentacle / Crossroad Press
The Job / Crossroad Press
The House on the Moor / Dark Regions Press
The Plasm / Dark Regions Press
Professor Challenger: The Island of Terror / Dark Regions Press
Sherlock Holmes: Revenant / Dark Regions Press

SHORT STORY COLLECTIONS

Inspector Lestrade: The Black Temple / Weird House Press
The Ghost Club / Crystal Lake Publishing
Dark Melodies / Dark Regions Press
Carnacki: Heaven and Hell / Dark Regions Press
Carnacki: The Watcher at the Gate / Dark Regions Press
Carnacki: The Edinburgh Townhouse / Lovecraft ezine
Carnacki: Starry Wisdom / Dark Regions Press
Sherlock Holmes: The Quality of Mercy / Dark Regions Press
Professor Challenger: The Kew Growths / Dark Regions Press
The Midnight Eye Files: Omnibus / Gryphonwood Press
The Midnight Eye Files: Omnibus 2 / Gryphonwood Press
Samurai and Other Stories / Crystal Lake Publishing
Myth and Monsters / KnightWatch Press

Curious about other Crossroad Press books? Stop by our
website: http://crossroadpress.com
We offer quality writing
in digital, audio, and print formats.

Subscribe to our newsletter on the website homepage and receive
a free eBook.